'carnation

The Many Lives of Ordell Clayton Hart

Matthew W Bertsch

BLOODBORNE PUBLISHING

Published by

Bloodborne Publishing

bloodbornepublishingllc@gmail.com

ISBN: 979-8-218-60962-7

Table of Contents

Acknowledgements

A book is never truly the work of one person, and this one is no exception. I am deeply grateful to the many individuals who helped bring this story to life.

To Richard L. Nunez, whose creative input during our screenplay brainstorming sessions laid the foundation for what this book would become – thank you for helping me see the potential in this story.

My heartfelt thanks to Randall Artherhults, my school-teacher and mentor in the creative arts, whose careful editing of this book and thoughtful insights helped shape not just the grammar but the very soul of this book. Your guidance in helping me connect with readers has been invaluable.

To my mother, Joyce Bertsch, whose wisdom and direction have always steered me true – thank you for being both my compass and my champion throughout this journey.

To my wife, Marcia Skersey – your unwavering support, encouragement, and editorial eye have been my constant companions through this process. This book exists because you believed in it, and in me.

I owe a special debt of gratitude to my morning coffee crew – Arnold Bailey, Dick Branam, Bill Arnold and Todd Bertsch (my brother). Our daily conversations kept my creative spirit alive, and your willingness to review drafts and offer feedback has been instrumental in bringing this book to completion.

And last, but certainly not least, I want to give special thanks to the 'Winemaker', who sometimes does things I'm not expecting and turns my vinegar into wine.

Without these remarkable individuals, this book would have remained nothing more than a dream. Each of you has left an indelible mark on these pages, and I am profoundly grateful for your contributions.

Preface

From Moonshine to Mercy: A Note from the Author

It all began in a garage in Texas when my friend, Richard L. Nunez, and I were sitting around, brainstorming up an idea for a movie.

As I recall, it was December in Dallas, a bit cold (relatively speaking to the rest of the nation). Hunting season was underway.

Now, I have no issues with hunting as long as the game is consumed and isn't simply beheaded and hung on a wall. I, myself, grew up hunting and, being frugal while in college, survived on harvested squirrels and rabbits from time to time.

Richard and I began regurgitating ideas about what sort of thoughts go through animal's minds when they're being hunted or stalked; what if the tables were turned?

Then the gears began in motion and I began writing out a screenplay; 'carnation was carnated.

What emerged was a profound exploration of redemption, second chances, and the extraordinary ways life teaches us its most valuable lessons.

Clay's journey — from a reckless exterminator with a fondness for homemade moonshine, to a man discovering the true meaning of compassion — mirrors the struggles many of us face. How often do we find ourselves stuck in patterns of behavior that harm not only those around us but our own souls as well? How many times must we hit rock bottom before we learn to look outward or upward?

Through Clay's misadventures as various creatures, he witnesses the world from new perspectives. He sees through the eyes of the very beings he once pursued with such reckless abandon. His transformations force him to experience life from different vantage points, challenging his preconceptions and slowly opening his heart to deeper truths.

But this isn't just a story about personal transformation. It's about the power of enduring love, represented by Maddie Warren, whose childhood letter becomes both symbol and catalyst for Clay's redemption. It's about friendship, embodied by Pastor Matt's unwavering support. And ultimately, it's about discovering that life itself is precious — every moment, every breath, every chance to make things right.

The title 'carnation plays on the concept of reincarnation, but with a twist that suggests rebirth and growth, much like the flower itself. Clay's journey through various animal forms isn't just about punishment or penance — it's about learning to see the world through new eyes, about understanding that every creature has its place in the grand design of life.

As you follow Clay's journey from self-destruction to salvation, I hope you'll find yourself reflecting on your own life's path (and maybe even have a laugh or two along the way).

Welcome to Clay's world. May his story remind you that sometimes the longest journey is the one from your head to your heart.

Matthew W Bertsch

December 2024

"'carnation: The Many Lives of Ordell Clayton Hart is a wildly original, laugh-out-loud journey of redemption, love, and second chances, blending Texas charm, heartfelt wisdom, and divine mischief in a story that's as touching as it is hilarious." – NewInBooks.com

'carnation

The Many Lives of Ordell Clayton Hart

1 - Critter Ridders

The Texas sun had barely cleared the horizon when the first complaint call came in. Ordell Clayton Hart — Clay to everyone who knew him — was already suited up and ready for action, his white van streaking through the sleepy suburbs like a missile with a mission. Queen's 'Another One Bites the Dust' blasted from the speakers, the heavy bass line matching his racing pulse.

"Time to rid the world of another menace," he muttered, his fingers drumming against the steering wheel. The magnetic sign on his van proclaimed 'CRITTER RIDDERS' in bold letters, the image of a cartoon exterminator giving a thumbs-up beneath.

Clay took the corners like a getaway driver, his van's single blue light casting eerie shadows across manicured lawns. A jogger, caught mid-stride at a crosswalk, dove into a median's bushes as Clay roared past, horn blaring. In his rearview mirror, Clay caught a glimpse of the woman's indignant gesture and grinned.

"Sorry, ma'am, but duty calls! Can't let them varmints get the upper hand!"

The flash of movement in his mirror reminded him to check for cops. Sure enough, up ahead, a patrol car lurked in its usual spot. Clay killed the light, dropped his speed to an innocent crawl, and turned down Queen until it was barely a whisper. He even managed a friendly wave as he passed the officer, the very picture of a law-abiding citizen.

Once clear, Clay cranked his tunes and gunned the engine again, the van's acceleration pushing him back in his seat. "Sweet Mercy, I love this job!"

The van squealed into the Oak Haven subdivision, rubber protesting as Clay took the final turn. He pulled up in front of a pristine two-story colonial, the kind of house where people probably ate dinner at a proper dining room table every night. Clay gave his reflection a quick once-over in the rearview mirror, adjusting his custom-made exterminator's helmet. The thing was his pride and joy — part motorcycle helmet, part space suit visor, with various homemade modifications he swore gave him "tactical advantages" in the field.

From his equipment bay, Clay assembled his gear with practiced efficiency. Each item on his utility belt had its specific purpose, though any rational person might question the need for a grappling hook when dealing with mice. His custom-built "critter gun" — a modified paintball marker that now shot tranquilizer darts — hung at his hip like a cowboy's six-shooter.

"Time to saddle up," he drawled, giving the gun a theatrical spin before holstering it. The weight of his equipment made him walk with a slight waddle, tools jingling like a death-metal wind chime with each step.

Clay marched up to the front door and pressed the doorbell, bouncing on the balls of his feet with barely contained energy. The door opened to reveal a well-dressed woman whose expression shifted from hopeful to bewildered as she took in Clay's appearance.

"Critter Ridders at yer service, ma'am" Clay announced, doffing his helmet with a flourish. "Name's Clay, and I'll be handlin' your pest situation today." He paused for dramatic effect. "Ma'am, you can rest easy now. The cavalry has arrived."

The woman blinked several times, as if hoping the vision before her might resolve itself into something more conventional. "It's ... it's just a little mouse," she managed finally, her voice barely above a whisper.

Clay's expression turned grave. "Just a mouse?" He leaned in close, lowering his voice to a conspiratorial whisper. "Ma'am, there ain't no such thing as 'just' a mouse. Where there's one, there's likely a whole army of 'em, plotting and scheming behind your walls. But don't you worry — that's why I'm here."

Without waiting for a response, Clay shouldered past her into the house, his gear clattering against the doorframe. The woman watched him go, her mouth still hanging open, as if she'd just invited a tornado into her living room.

She wasn't entirely wrong.

Inside the immaculate home, Clay launched into his standard operating procedure — which was anything but standard. He dropped to his hands and knees, pressing his ear to the baseboard like a safe-cracker listening for tumbler clicks.

"Ah-ha!" he exclaimed, startling the homeowner who'd been nervously hovering nearby. "Just as I suspected. Classic infestation pattern, probably started in the fall of '22." He looked up at her with deadly seriousness. "You can tell by the way they're scratchin'. Yep, I reckon they started building their fortress around September ... no, October of '22."

The woman's polite smile grew strained. "I only saw the one mouse. Yesterday. In the kitchen."

Clay waved off her amateur assessment as he began setting an elaborate array of traps along the baseboards. "Trust me, ma'am, I'm a professional. What you're dealin' with here is probably a whole syndicate. Organized crime, rodent division."

As he worked, Clay muttered to himself about proper trap spacing and "tactical coverage zones." His concentration was so intense that when one trap snapped shut on his finger, he barely noticed — at first.

"SWEET MERCY!" he yelped, jumping to his feet and shaking his hand. "These new models got some real bite to 'em!" He turned to the homeowner with a forced grin. "Don't worry, ma'am, just testing the tension. Gotta make sure they're calibrated exactly right."

The woman pressed her lips together, clearly fighting the urge to suggest he call the whole thing off. But before she could speak, a flash of grey darted across the kitchen floor.

Clay's entire demeanor changed in an instant. Gone was the bumbling exterminator, replaced by something closer to a Special Forces operator. He drew his critter gun in one fluid motion, years of watching action movies evident in his stance.

"Ma'am, I'm gonna have to ask you to step back," he said, his voice dropping an octave. "This could get ugly."

Without warning, Clay spun around, accidentally backing into the homeowner. His protective gesture went awry, his hand nearly landing somewhere far more personal than intended. The woman gasped — whether from the contact or from the sight of the ridiculously large dart gun, it wasn't clear.

"Shh," Clay whispered, too focused on his target to notice the social faux pas. "There he is."

The mouse, perhaps sensing the gravity of the situation, made a break for the window. It scurried up the counter with impressive agility, squeezed through a small hole in the screen, and disappeared into the backyard.

Clay lowered his weapon slowly, his expression unreadable behind his visor. Then, like a switch being flipped, he burst into action.

"Perfect!" he shouted, startling the homeowner yet again. "Didn't want to make a mess of your nice clean walls anyway. All part of the plan — we're taking this outside!"

Before the homeowner could protest, Clay was charging toward her sliding glass door, his gear rattling like a one-man band in full swing. His enthusiasm for the chase nearly cost him dearly as he almost ran face-first into the glass, catching himself at the last second with a squeak of his gloved hand against the surface.

"Don't worry, ma'am," he called over his shoulder as he fumbled with the door handle. "This is where the real magic happens. Outdoor pursuits are my specialty!"

Under her breath, the woman muttered something that sounded suspiciously like, "That's what I'm afraid of."

Out in the backyard, Clay paused to get his bearings. The morning sun cast long shadows across a pristine garden that looked like it had come straight from the pages of Better Homes & Gardens. Clay's trained eye immediately identified at least seventeen potential mouse hiding spots, twelve possible escape routes, and one very unfortunate garden gnome that was about to have a really bad day.

A rustle in the flower bed caught his attention. Without hesitation, Clay snatched up a shovel that had been leaning against the house. He tested its weight with a few practice swings that would have made a golf pro cringe.

"Say yer prayers, rodent!" he bellowed, channeling his inner action hero.

What followed could only be described as choreographed chaos. Clay launched into a series of wild shovel swings that seemed inspired equally by tennis, hockey, and what he probably thought ninja fighting looked like. Each miss at his target sent dirt, mulch, and unfortunately-placed garden decorations flying in all directions.

Through the sliding glass door, the homeowner watched in horror as her carefully cultivated flower beds became collateral damage in Clay's one-man war on rodents. Her prized petunias went airborne, her wind chimes performed their swan song, and her collection of decorative garden stakes became impromptu javelins as Clay's enthusiasm got the better of his aim.

The mouse, meanwhile, demonstrated a survival instinct worthy of a chess grandmaster, always managing to be precisely where Clay's shovel wasn't. It darted along the fence line, leading Clay on a merry chase that resembled nothing so much as a slapstick comedy routine.

"Come back here and face me like a man!" Clay shouted, his dignity abandoning him entirely as he tripped over a garden hose and nearly face-planted into a bird bath.

The mouse paused just long enough to seem almost contemplative before squeezing under the fence into the neighbor's yard. Clay, his chest heaving and his uniform now decorated with an impressive collection of grass stains, eyed the fence with grim determination.

"So that's how you wanna play it, huh?" he muttered, adjusting his helmet which had gone slightly askew during his acrobatics. "Well, two can play at that game."

Clay's first attempt to scale the fence resulted in what could generously be described as a learning experience. His equipment belt caught on a picket, leaving him dangling like a Christmas ornament until he managed to extract himself with as much dignity as he could muster — which wasn't much.

"Tactical retreat," he mumbled, brushing off his uniform. His eyes lit up as he spotted a gate a few feet away. "Ah-ha! The element of surprise!"

He crept toward the gate with all the stealth of a tap-dancing elephant, his gear jingling with every exaggerated tiptoe. As he rounded the corner into his neighbor's yard, Clay found himself face-to-face with a scene of suburban tranquility: a couple enjoying their morning coffee on their patio.

The mouse, with impeccable timing, chose that moment to sprint across their table.

Clay, operating purely on instinct and questionable judgment, launched into action. The couple's peaceful morning dissolved into chaos as he dove across their patio, shovel swinging wildly. An empty chair went sailing through the air, bouncing off the house's brick wall with a clatter that probably registered on local seismographs.

The wife's shriek of terror pierced the morning air. Clay paused mid-pursuit, remembering his professional credentials. He fumbled for his ID badge, holding it up like a shield.

"I know, they're scary, aren't they?" he said with complete sincerity, as if his badge explained everything about why a grown man in modified sports equipment was destroying their patio furniture.

Before they could respond, Clay was off again, in hot pursuit of his quarry. He rounded the corner of their house, his breathing heavy but his determination unwavering.

As he crept along the wall, he passed by an open window and caught an unexpected glimpse of a young woman fastening her bra. Their eyes met in the window glass. Her scream of surprise was followed immediately by Clay's awkward attempt at damage control.

"No worries!" he called out, tipping his helmet in what he hoped was a gentlemanly fashion. "Official brassiere-ness, uh .... " He stumbled over the words before finally managing, "Official business, ma'am. Stay in the house."

Clay's face burned beneath his visor as he continued his pursuit. "Sweet mercy," he muttered to himself, "why do these things always happen to me?"

Peeking around the corner of the house, he spotted the mouse scampering in his direction. With the speed born of countless hours practicing in his backyard — much to his neighbors' ongoing concern — Clay whipped out his homemade "spike strip" from his utility belt.

The device, which was really just a series of mousetraps connected with duct tape and optimism, sailed through the air with all the grace of a thrown brick. It landed perfectly in the mouse's path — and failed spectacularly as the rodent simply changed direction, leaving Clay staring at his invention in betrayal.

The mouse's retreat triggered another wild chase, punctuated by crashes, bangs, and what sounded suspiciously like another garden gnome meeting an untimely end. From overhead, the path of destruction traced through the suburban landscape like a deranged connect-the-dots puzzle, leading through no fewer than six backyards, each one bearing Clay's unique brand of chaos.

"This would be so much easier if people would just coordinate their fence heights," Clay grumbled as he belly-crawled under a particularly low gate, his equipment leaving a rut in the grass behind him.

The pursuit finally led him back to his starting point, leaving Clay covered in dirt, grass stains, and what he desperately hoped was mud from someone's vegetable garden; though it exuded an essence of 'natural' fertilizer. Whether its source was from a dog or a cow, he couldn't quite decipher, but his once-pristine uniform now looked like he'd gone ten rounds in a mud-wrestling pit.

The original homeowner stood on her front porch, mouth agape at the destruction that radiated out from her yard like ripples in a pond. Before she could speak, Clay held up a professional finger.

"All part of the service, ma'am," he wheezed, trying to catch his breath while maintaining his dignity. "Standard pursuit protocol. We'll, uh ... we'll get him next time."

The mouse, as if to put a final exclamation point on Clay's defeat, darted between his legs and disappeared into a storm drain.

Clay watched it go, his shoulders slumping slightly before he caught himself and straightened up. "Well," he announced, brushing ineffectually at his uniform, "looks like this little fella's gonna need the deluxe package. I'll draw up the paperwork and get you an estimate for our comprehensive rodent elimination program."

The homeowner's face went through an impressive array of emotions before settling on polite panic. "Oh, no, that's ... that's quite all right. I think you've done more than enough."

"But ma'am," Clay protested, "you can't just leave a situation like this half-handled. Why, that mouse could be back with reinforcements! You need someone with experience, someone with dedication, someone with...."

"I'll call an exterminator!" she blurted out.

Clay drew himself up to his full height, offended to his core. "Ma'am, I *am* an exterminator."

"A ... different one," she clarified gently.

Clay opened his mouth to argue further, but something in her expression told him this was one battle he wasn't going to win. He sighed, reaching into his belt for a business card that had somehow survived the morning's adventure.

"Well, if you change your mind, " He handed her the card with as much ceremony as he could muster. "Critter Ridders is always here to serve. No varmint too small, no pursuit too challenging."

As Clay trudged back to his van, he noticed several neighbors looking out their windows while on their cells, no doubt leading to some interesting conversations with their insurance companies. He slid behind the wheel, started the engine, and cranked up "Another One Bites the Dust" to drown out the sound of approaching sirens in the distance.

"Some days," he mused, pulling away from the curb, "you get the varmint. And some days," He glanced in his rearview mirror at the chaos he was leaving behind. "Some days the varmint gets you."

But there was always tomorrow. And somewhere out there, another critter was waiting to be rid. Clay smiled, already looking forward to his next adventure.

Even if his insurance company wasn't.

2 - Lost Connections

The Primrose Café nestled in the heart of Christchurch like a warm secret, its weathered brick exterior softened by climbing jasmine and morning glory. Inside, sunlight streamed through tall windows, catching tiny orbs of dust that danced above freshly wiped tables and created glimmers above the steam rising from coffee cups.

Maddie Warren traced the rim of her pearl cup with an absent finger, lost in the kind of thoughts that only surface when you're on the cusp of changing your life. Across the table, her best friend, Emma, watched her with the keen eye of someone who'd weathered a decade of friendship's storms.

"Penny for your thoughts?" Emma's voice carried that particular Kiwi accent that Maddie had grown to love during her years in New Zealand. "You've been a million miles away since you decided to take that research position back in the States."

Maddie sighed, tucking an errant curl behind her ear. The gesture, unconscious and familiar, reminded Emma of all the times she'd watched her friend fidget through decisions both mundane and monumental.

"I know it's the right move," Maddie said finally. "Going back to Dad's old university, continuing some of his work .... " She trailed off, her gaze drifting to the window where a tūī bird was performing aerial acrobatics among the flowering kōwhai trees.

"But?" Emma prompted, leaning forward. The morning sun caught the silver pendant at her throat, sending little flashes of light across their table.

"I've just been thinking about someone lately." Maddie's voice softened, taking on a quality Emma hadn't heard before. "Someone from back in Texas."

Emma's eyes lit up with interest. "Oh? Do tell!"

A smile tugged at the corners of Maddie's mouth, equal parts sweet and sad. "His name was Ordell Clayton Hart, but everyone called him Clay." She laughed softly, the sound rich with memory. "He was this absolutely fearless little boy with the biggest heart I'd ever known. Never met a challenge he wouldn't tackle head-on, even if it meant landing flat on his face."

As Maddie spoke, her acquired accent shifted subtly, Texas bleeding through her carefully cultivated professional tone. Emma watched, fascinated, as years seemed to fall away from her friend's face.

"We were thick as thieves back then," Maddie continued, warmth coloring her voice. "Always running around getting into the best kind of trouble. He had this way of making everything fun, an adventure, even if we were just playing in his backyard."

Emma watched her friend's face soften, noted the way her fingers had stilled on her coffee cup. Whoever this Clay was, he'd clearly left an impression that time hadn't managed to fade.

14

"How, after all these years of knowing you, you've never mentioned him before," Emma observed carefully.

Maddie hadn't mentioned him before; perhaps the knife cut too deep to reopen that wound again.

Emma pressed further, "Must have been someone special to have you looking like that after all these years."

Maddie blinked, coming back to herself. "Like what?"

"Like you just found something precious you thought you'd lost forever."

Maddie traced a drop of condensation down the side of her cup, her mind wandering back to sunbaked Texas afternoons and a scheming grin that could light up a room.

"We were in 4-H together," she said, smiling at Emma's puzzled expression. "It's like ... imagine if Elon Musk met Lucille Ball, had a baby, and that baby was determined to teach every other kid in the club how to build an automated carwash for farm animals."

Emma laughed, the sound mingling with the gentle clatter of cups and saucers from the café's busy counter. "Sounds terrifying."

"Oh, it was! But Clay, " Maddie's eyes took on that faraway look again. "Clay made everything fun. He'd name all the animals these ridiculous things – called his sheep 'Sir Woolington, the Third' even though it was definitely a female. And when it came time for competitions, he'd get so excited he'd practically vibrate out of his boots."

She paused, caught in the memory. "He never won first place – or any place, really. But it never seemed to bother him. He'd just dust himself off, flash that infectious grin of his, and declare that next time would be his moment of glory."

"Sounds like quite the character," Emma observed, signaling the waiter for a coffee refill. "What happened between you two?"

The question hung in the air like morning mist, heavy with unspoken possibilities. Maddie's smile faded slightly.

"Life, I suppose. Dad's work brought us back here to New Zealand, and you know how it is at that age. We promised to write, to stay in touch. " She shrugged, but the casualness of the gesture felt forced. "I left him with a letter, right before we left. Poured my whole heart into it, told him how much his friendship meant to me, how special he was."

"And?" Emma prompted gently.

"And nothing; never heard back." Maddie straightened in her chair, squaring her shoulders against an old hurt. "I mean, we were just kids. Probably for the best – you know how childhood sweethearts usually turn out."

But Emma wasn't buying the breezy dismissal. She'd known Maddie too long, had seen her friend navigate relationships with careful precision, always maintaining a safe emotional distance. Now, watching Maddie's fingers worry at her napkin, Emma wondered if she was finally seeing the reason why.

"Have you thought about looking him up?" she asked carefully. "Now that you're heading back?"

"What? No, that would be .... " Maddie started to protest, but her voice trailed off. After a moment, she admitted, "Maybe. I've caught myself wondering what became of him. He had such a gift with animals

– this innate understanding of them. I always thought he'd end up working at a shelter or rescue organization."

"Or maybe he became a rugged Texas rancher," Emma teased, waggling her eyebrows. "Living that cowboy life, breaking hearts across the Lone Star State."

Maddie rolled her eyes, but a faint blush colored her cheeks. "More likely he's married with a house full of kids and pets; living that perfect rural life with a vast, barbed-wire fence and Sunday barbecues."

"Or," Emma said, leaning forward with a conspiratorial grin, "he's been pining for his childhood sweetheart all these years, wondering why she never wrote him again."

"Wrote *him*? *He* never wrote *me*," Maddie proclaimed, with a tone mixed somewhere between anger and disappointment.

"I .... " She pressed her fingers to her temples, trying to organize her thoughts. "I left him with that letter. I...it had our new address, our phone number – everything he'd need to keep in touch."

Emma set her coffee down, giving Maddie her full attention. "And?"

"And nothing. Never heard back." Maddie swallowed hard. "I waited for weeks, kept checking the mail every day. I even tried calling once, but international calls were so expensive back then, and when no one answered .... " She shrugged, but the casualness of the gesture felt forced.

"You thought he'd moved on," Emma finished softly. "Found new friends, new interests ... left the past in the past."

"Well, wouldn't you?" Maddie's voice carried a defensive edge. "We were young. Life changes. People change."

"Some things don't change," Emma countered, her tone gentle but firm. "The way your eyes lit up when you finally just told me about him? That's not nothing, Mads."

Maddie opened her mouth to argue, then closed it again. The waiter approached with Emma's refill, and they sat in companionable silence as he topped off their cups. The rich aroma of fresh coffee swirled between them, carrying with it memories of other conversations, other crossroads.

"He ... he was special," Maddie admitted finally, her voice barely above a whisper. "Not just to me – to everyone. He just had this ... light about him. This incredible capacity for joy, even when things went wrong."

"You know," Emma said carefully, "it's funny how we sometimes build stories in our minds to explain things we don't understand. How we take one outcome and construct whole narratives around it, never considering there might be other possibilities."

Maddie stared into her coffee cup, watching cream swirl in abstract patterns. "What are you saying?"

"I'm saying maybe it's time to question some of your assumptions." Emma reached across the table, squeezing her friend's hand. "You're going back to Texas anyway. What's the harm in looking him up?"

"And say what?" Maddie's laugh held a brittle edge. "'Hey, remember me? The girl who disappeared from your life twenty years ago? Just wondering why you never wrote me back!'"

"How about, 'Hey, remember me? The girl who never forgot you, even after all these years?'" Emma's voice softened. "The girl who still smiles when she talks about you?"

18

The café had begun to empty, lunch crowds giving way to the quiet lull of mid-afternoon. Maddie watched a pair of university students pack up their laptops at a nearby table, their easy laughter reminding her of simpler times.

"You know what's funny?" she said, absently stirring her now-cold coffee. "I used to imagine running into him somewhere. Some random airport or conference. He'd be this brilliant veterinarian or world-famous animal behaviorist, and we'd laugh about how we both ended up following the same path."

Emma tilted her head. "And now?"

"Now?" Maddie's lips curved in a self-deprecating smile. "Now I'm wondering if I've built him up in my head; made him into this perfect memory that no reality could possibly match."

"Or maybe," Emma suggested, "you're just scared of finding out the truth – whatever that might be."

The words hung in the air between them, too accurate to dismiss. Outside, clouds scudded across the New Zealand sky, their shadows racing across the café's worn wooden floors.

"You know, they used to have this saying in Texas," Maddie said suddenly, seemingly unrelated, but it would lead to a point. At Emma's puzzled look, she explained, "They used to say: 'Everyone wants to go to heaven, but no one wants to die to get there.'"

Emma raised an eyebrow. "That's rather morbid for a casual coffee chat, isn't it?"

"No, no – hear me out." Maddie leaned forward, warming to her theme. "It wasn't really about death at all. It was about how we all want things from life – happiness, success, fulfillment – but we're not always willing to make sacrifices to get them. We want the reward without the struggle — the risk."

Understanding dawned in Emma's eyes. "And you think that's what you've been doing? Playing it safe?"

"Maybe." Maddie glanced out the window, watching a young couple share an umbrella as the first drops of rain began to fall. "When Dad got the offer to come back to New Zealand, part of me was relieved. It was easier to leave than to face how much Clay meant to me. Easier to write one letter and tell myself he'd moved on than to keep trying, keep reaching out."

"But now?"

"Now .... " Maddie straightened in her chair, something shifting in her expression. "Now I'm going back. And maybe it's time to stop playing it safe. To find out what really happened to that letter — to Clay."

"To the girl who wrote it," Emma finished softly.

Maddie nodded, a familiar determination settling over her features. Emma had seen that look before – it usually preceded some of her friend's most significant life decisions.

"He probably won't even remember me," Maddie said, but the words lacked conviction.

Emma snorted. "Right. Because everyone forgets their first love. The person who saw them at their most authentic, most alive." She reached for the check, waving away Maddie's protest. "Consider this my investment in your romantic redemption arc."

"It's not – I mean, I'm not expecting .... " Maddie fumbled for words, a rare occurrence for someone usually so articulate.

"You've been reading too many romance novels," Maddie groaned, but she was smiling.

They said their goodbyes, Emma extracting one final promise that Maddie wouldn't chicken out of looking for Clay once she got to Texas. As Maddie drove home through the rain-washed streets of Christchurch, her mind wandered back to that last day in Texas, to the letter she'd pressed into Clay's hands.

Now, twenty years later, Maddie felt that same surge of emotion as she turned onto her street. Something was pulling her back to Texas, back to the mystery of that unanswered letter, back to Clay.

"Time to find out what really happened," she whispered to herself, determination settling over her like a familiar coat.

"Time to find you, Clay Hart."

3 - The Critter Commando

Clay was on the road again, cruising in his Critter Ridders van and still stinging from his latest mousecapade. Suddenly, a little pug romping in a suburban yard caught his eye.

"Well, well, well, what have we here?" Clay squinted at the pup, which was gleefully shredding a plush toy, white fluff dangling from its jaws. "A stray! Rabid by the looks of it. Foaming at the mouth and all!"

Clay stomped the brakes, the van lurching to a stop. Swapping his exterminator cap for an official 'Dog Catcher' number, he hopped out and also swapped out his van's magnetic signage, now proudly displaying 'K9 Catchers'. Stealthily, he approached the pint-sized 'menace'.

"Don't you worry, little doggie," Clay smirked as he unclipped a canister of mace from his utility belt. "Ole Clay's gonna take real good care of ya."

Just then, the pooch spotted Clay and started yipping excitedly. It bounded playfully toward him, fluffy tail wagging, ready to make a new friend.

Suddenly, a woman burst from the house, dashing towards them. "Brutus! Come!"

The dog scampered to its owner, who scooped it up protectively. "What on earth are you doing? That's my pup!"

Clay whipped out a notepad and pen, standing as officially as possible despite his questionable authority. He flipped through several pages covered in hasty scrawls until he found a blank one.

"Now, Section 4, Paragraph B of the municipal code clearly states .... " He paused, realizing he had no idea what the actual code says. Still, he began writing with exaggerated seriousness, his tongue poking out slightly in concentration.

The woman's eyes began to well up as she clutched Brutus closer. "Are you writing me a ticket? Please, I've had such a hard day already."

Clay's pen continued its relentless scrawling, his tongue poking out slightly in concentration as he filled in every line of the citation with deliberate thoroughness.

"Sir, please," the lady pleaded, "I'm already having a rough time with the bills. How much is this gonna cost me anyway?"

Clay didn't even look up from his writing. "Two hundred and fifty dollars, plus court costs if you wanna fight it." He tore the ticket from his pad with theatrical flourish and thrust it toward her. "Hopefully enough that you'll keep that little menace locked up where he belongs."

The woman's face crumpled as she stared at the citation. "Two hundred and fifty? But I... I can't afford..."

Clay interrupted, adjusting his utility belt with smug satisfaction. "Look, little Peter Lorre there coulda darted out into the road and killed

26

someone - caused an accident or somethin'! Law's the law, lady. I ain't got no sympathy for irresponsible pet owners."

Clay tipped his hat sarcastically, then retreated to his van before the situation could escalate into another backyard debacle.

The woman pulled her pup in for a tight squeeze, comforting him. "It's OK, Brutus, we'll get through this ... somehow," she sniffled as Clay peeled away, "Guess we gotta be more careful. This world is full of crazy, hateful people."

Feeling a bit frazzled from his morning misadventures, Clay decided he was thirsty. Noon on a Tuesday wasn't too early for a beer, right? Spotting a place called 'The Garden', he swung the van into an alley and marched in, ready to wet his whistle. He took a second glance at the bar's name on the door as he entered, "Goofy name for a bar, but as long as the beer is cold, I reckon they can call themself whatever they want."

Posting up at the bar, Clay ordered a frosty one and settled in to watch the game. A few stools down, a chipper fella in hospital scrubs eyed Clay's exterminator uniform with poorly concealed disapproval.

"So, you like baseball?" the man asked, his voice carefully neutral.

Clay barely glanced over, focused on the TV. "Sure do. Nothing like watching the boys of summer swinging some heavy lumber around."

"Indeed." The man scooted closer. "Name's Bruce. I'm a nurse down at Methodist. I also volunteer at the animal sanctuary on weekends."

Clay, oblivious and more interested in the game than chatting, scanned the bar for some snacks. No luck.

"Hey barkeep, you got some nuts I can munch on?" Clay hollered. "Or better yet, you got any pork rinds? I need somethin' salty!"

Bruce couldn't help but comment. "They have these amazing roasted chickpeas here. Much better for you than processed junk. Especially when you're on your feet all day like we are."

Swallowing his current gulp, Clay perked up at the notion. "Chickpeas? What in tarnation? A bar's supposed to have nuts and beef jerky!" He pointed at the TV. "Oh c'mon, he was safe!"

Clay smacked his lips and rubbed his belly. "Hey, barkeep, can you rustle me up some hot wings? I'm starvin' over here."

"We have some buffalo cauliflower; they're delicious. And not only are they healthier, they're humane."

Clay, still absorbed in the game, shakes his head in disbelief, "What kinda bar ain't got no wings?"

Bruce's expression hardened a bit as he noticed the "Critter Ridders" logo on Clay's vest. "So, you're an exterminator, huh? I don't suppose you use live traps and just relocate them; you know, win-win for everyone?"

The accusation finally caught Clay's attention. He squinted at the man, then did a slow pan of the bar – a couple men in a booth with yoga mats propped next to them, the wheatgrass shots being served, the "Go Vegan!" posters on the walls. Clay nearly choked on his beer.

"Sweet Mercy!" Clay sputtered, the puzzle pieces snapping into place. He fumbled for his wallet, tossed a crumpled fiver on the bar, and beat a hasty retreat. "Knock yourselves out, all the more burgers for me!"

As Clay exited, Bruce turned to the bartender and chuckled. "Well, there goes another one. You know, in our ER they patch up all of God's creatures — even the ones who don't regard them."

Back on the road, Clay white-knuckled the steering wheel, eager to put as much distance as possible between himself and 'The Garden'. He cranked up the radio, trying to drown out the memory of his wasted time with those extremists.

Up ahead, a squirrel inched out into the road. Clay swerved, attempting to rid the world of another disease-infested rodent. He glanced in the rearview mirror, hoping to see a puff of fur and a tiny, flattened body. No such luck.

"Ha! I'll git ya next time, rodent!" Clay cackled; his eyes still glued to the mirror.

A blaring horn snapped his attention back to the road. Clay's eyes bulged as he realized he'd drifted into the oncoming lane, and was now playing chicken with a massive semi-truck.

"Sweet mercy!" Clay yelped, jerking the wheel hard to the right. The van careened off the road, bouncing through the ditch and coming to a shuddering stop in a cloud of dust.

For a moment, Clay just sat there, heart pounding, trying to catch his breath. He gave himself a quick once-over, checking for injuries. Miraculously, he seemed to be in one piece. The van, on the other hand ....

Clay hopped out to survey the damage. It didn't take a mechanic to see that his faithful steed was down for the count. The front axle was snapped clean in half, and smoke poured from the crumpled hood.

"Well, ain't that just a kick in the giblets," Clay sighed, giving the tire a halfhearted kick; stuck in a ditch, no cell phone, not a soul in sight. He was well and truly stranded.

With a resigned groan, Clay started walking, thumb outstretched in the universal sign of a hitchhiker. It was going to be a long trek home. And to think, the day started with such promise.

As the sun beat down and the miles stretched on, Clay found himself longing for the simple comforts of home: a cold drink, a soft couch, a break from the nonstop craziness of his chosen profession.

At this point, he'd almost prefer another round with that frisky mouse. Almost. But Clay was nothing if not resilient. He'd get through this, just like he always did; one painful step at a time.

And hey, at least out here, hoofing it on the open road, there were no cabbage-fartin' do-gooders or pugnacious pups to contend with; just Clay, his thoughts, and the long, dusty trail ahead.

For now, that would have to do.

4 - A Moonshine Mishap

The Texas sun hung low on the horizon like a disappointed parent watching Clay stumble up the gravel drive to his ramshackle house. Every muscle in his body protested the day's misadventures, his clothes were caked with the particular kind of dust that only comes from lying in a ditch contemplating one's life choices, and his throat felt like he'd been gargling a sandbox. But he was home now. These days, that was about the best he could hope for.

Inside, Clay made an unsteady beeline for the fridge, yanking it open with more force than necessary. The rush of cool air hit his face as he grabbed a beer, cracking it open and draining half in one desperate chug. The liquid was a blessed relief as it slid down his parched throat, though a small voice in the back of his mind — one that sounded suspiciously like mom — reminded him that water might have been the wiser choice.

"Sweet mercy, what a day," he muttered, wiping his mouth with the back of his hand. His eyes drifted to the calendar tacked crookedly on the wall, and suddenly the day's disasters didn't seem quite so important. A slow grin spread across his face as realization dawned.

Today was the day. After months of tweaking and tending, his prized creation — 'Hound's Tooth Moonshine' — would finally be ready for sampling.

Clay set his beer aside, smacked and rubbed his hands together with gleeful anticipation. He'd been working on this batch for months, adjusting the recipe, fiddling with the still, getting everything just right. If his calculations were correct — and when weren't they, at least in his own mind — this would be his finest vintage yet.

The shed in his backyard that housed his makeshift distillery beckoned like a temple of forbidden delights. Clay hurried out back, the screen door banging shut behind him with a protest of rusty springs. The air inside the shed was thick with the pungent aroma of fermenting corn mash — a smell that would have made most people recoil but to Clay was sweeter than any perfume.

He grabbed a weathered 5-gallon bucket from a shelf lined with dozens of mason jars, holding it under the spigot like a beekeeper collecting the season's first, precious honey. The clear liquid gurgled out, filling the bucket with his prized creation. Once full, Clay dipped a mason jar into the potent brew, admiring the way the light that snuck through the gaps in the weathered boards played across its surface.

"Lookin' good," he murmured, swirling the jar with the affected sophistication of a wine connoisseur. "Lookin' reaaalll good."

The rich aroma hit him and even Clay's recovering cotton-mouth couldn't help but water at the fumes. They were strong enough to strip paint — which, in Clay's professional opinion, was exactly how good moonshine should be.

"Sweet mercy!" He blinked rapidly, his eyes stinging from the fumes. "That's got some kick!"

He raised the jar in a mock toast to his reflection in the grimy window. "Well, here's to y'all, you ornery critters. This one's for all the trouble you've caused me today."

And with that declaration of defiance against the universe at large, Clay tipped the jar back and took a hearty swig.

The moonshine hit his throat like liquid lightning, a white-hot blade of pure alcohol that seemed determined to burn its way straight through to his soul. Clay's eyes bulged as his face cycled through an impressive array of colors, finally settling on a shade of purple that medical professionals would have found concerning. His hands flew to his throat as he fought for air, certain that his last act on Earth would be choking to death on his own bootleg booze.

For a moment — one eternal, crystalline moment — Clay was convinced he might actually breathe fire. The room spun around him like a carnival ride designed by a sadist, and he could have sworn he saw his life flash before his eyes. But then, just as suddenly as it started, the sensation changed. The burn transformed into a warm glow that spread from his belly to his fingertips and rapidly cleared his sinuses, wrapping him in a cocoon of liquid courage.

"Sweet ... Mercy," Clay wheezed, a dopey grin spreading across his face. "That must be like ... 200 octane!" He paused, evaluating, "It's perfect!"

Clay took another sip, more cautiously this time, savoring the way the 'shine seemed to light him up from the inside out. All the aches and pains from his adventures of the day melted away, washed aside by a tide of liquid courage. Somewhere in the back of his mind, a small voice suggested that maybe he ought to pace himself; that this was powerful stuff, not to be trifled with. But the more he drank, the quieter that voice became.

He wandered back outside, mason jar bobbing precariously in his grip as he weaved his way to a pair of lawn chairs that served as his back porch furniture. The whole world had taken on a pleasant, fuzzy glow. Colors seemed brighter, sounds more muted. Even the relentless Texas heat felt less oppressive somehow.

The crunch of gravel pulled his attention to the driveway, where a familiar figure was making his way up the path. Tall and lanky, with a tinge of graying hair and a face weathered by sun and time — and, Clay suspected, the trials of shepherding a flock that included himself.

"Well, well! If it ain't the varmint vigilante himself!" Pastor Matt called out, a hint of amusement in his voice.

Clay struggled to focus, squinting against the setting sun. "Pastor Matt? That really you, or has my 'shine started workin' its magic already?"

The aging man chuckled, coming to a stop a few feet away. His eyes took in the scene — the mason jar, Clay's disheveled appearance, the general air of celebration-meets-desperation. "Thought I'd swing by and see how you were faring." He nodded towards the jar. "Though I'm guessing the critters drove you to drink, eh?"

Clay lurched to his feet, swaying slightly as he tried to find his balance. "Nah, nah, this here's just a little something I cooked up myself." He thrust the jar towards the pastor, sloshing some onto the grass. "A little taste of liquid relaxation, if you will. Care for a nip?"

Pastor Matt eyed the jar like it might bite him. "I'm not sure that's such a good idea, Clay. Looks like you've had enough for both of us already."

"Aw, c'mon now!" Clay protested, his words starting to blur at the edges. "Don't be such a mick in the stud! This is the good stuff, right here. Put hair on your chest and steel in your spine!"

The pastor looked like he was about to refuse, but then something flickered across his expression. A glint of mischief, perhaps. Or maybe just a touch of that old-time religion that said sometimes the best way to save a soul was to meet it where it lived.

"Alright, alright. One sip couldn't hurt, I suppose." He reached for the jar, examining it in the fading light. "To your health, Clay."

With that, Pastor Matt raised the jar and took what Clay would later describe as "a proper Christian swig." The effect was immediate and electric. The pastor's eyes popped, his face turning an alarming shade of crimson. He doubled over, coughing and sputtering as the moonshine blazed its unholy trail down his throat.

"Lake of fire and damnation!" he gasped, thrusting the jar back at Clay. "That's not moonshine, that's rocket fuel!"

Clay cackled with delight, slapping his knee. "Told ya it was the good stuff! Have a seat, Pastor. Let it settle in. First sip's always the hardest — like salvation, right?"

Pastor Matt sank into the empty chair, still trying to catch his breath. "I don't recall that particular comparison in my seminary studies," he managed, but his lips twitched with suppressed amusement.

They sat in silent harmony, watching the stars sprouting from the darkening sky. Clay took another pull from the jar, then offered it to the pastor, who waved it off with a shudder.

Clay respectfully withdrew the offer; all the better, more for himself. Not to be rude, though, to his only friend, he fetched a cold beer from the cooler next to his seat and tossed it to the pastor.

Clay let his head fall back to look into the vast majesty of space above. Then the self-damning thoughts started to creep in.

"You're the only friend I got," Clay said suddenly, the words tumbling out before he could catch them.

"Why do you say that?"

"'Cuz it's true." Clay looked back down and stared into the jar, as if it might hold answers to questions he hadn't even figured out how to ask. "I'm a real bastard."

"That's the 'shine talking," Pastor Matt said gently, then redirected. "Yeah, we all have our issues, but there's plenty to like about you."

Clay snorted, but there was more pain than humor in the sound. "Like what?"

"For one, you're a funny guy. A little edgy at times, but you've got a real quick wit about you. That's a sign of intelligence."

A flicker of something — pride, maybe, or embarrassment — crossed Clay's face before his defenses slammed back into place. "You're just sayin' that 'cause you're a pastor and you're tryin' to save me or somethin'."

Pastor Matt shook his head, settling deeper into his chair. "I can't save you, Clay. And you're not some special assignment to me; not a project. You're my neighbor, and you're a funny guy. Full of life."

"I hate life," Clay muttered, his voice thick with more than just moonshine. "It don't make no sense."

"You hate it?" Pastor Matt's eyes traveled to the jar in Clay's hands. "Tell me, how's the moonshine?"

Clay blinked wide-eyed at the perceived irrelevance. "What? What that got to do with the trice of pea in ... chice of tree ... what that got to do with anything?"

The pastor let out one of those unexpected laughs at Clay's linguistic gymnastics. It was one of those laughs where a small glob of spit unexpectedly pops out of your mouth and dangles from your chin like a climber repelling from a mountainside. Matt confirmed, while cleaning up with his sleeve, "Ha! See, it's good, isn't it?"

"Huh?"

"The drink. It's good. Life is good. Life is precious." Pastor Matt gestured expansively at the yard around them, then up to the heavens. "I would even argue that *everything* is good. It's just that sometimes good things can get twisted."

Clay's face darkened. "Life ain't no good! Can't you 'member all my stuff what happened to me? You were there." His voice cracked slightly. "Next you'll be sayin' everything happens for a reason."

Pastor Matt paused, weighing his words carefully. The moment stretched between them like a thread ready to snap. Finally, he said, "Well, I will say that nothing takes God by surprise. Mary and Joseph would have never been able to throw their kid a surprise birthday party, that's for sure."

Clay slammed down his jar hard enough to make the moonshine slosh. "It's gettin' late and you had too much to drink," he growled, trying to shut down the conversation before it ventured into territory too painful to navigate.

The pastor glanced pointedly at his barely-touched beer, then at Clay's significantly depleted mason jar, but kept his peace. "Yeah, I probably should be getting back." He stood, brushing off his pants. "Maybe you can come over for dinner later this week?"

Clay mumbled something noncommittal, his eyes fixed on the moonlit shadows.

"Well, thanks for the good drink and good company." Pastor Matt's voice was gentle. "You're a good neighbor, Clay. Let me know if you ever need anything."

As the pastor made his way out through the side gate and into his own backyard, Clay tipped back his jar, shaking the last drop of moonshine into his mouth. The world was really starting to spin now, the edges of reality going soft and blurry. He leaned his head back again, staring at the stars through the bottom of the empty glass.

"They sure don't make pitchers as big as they used to," he muttered to himself.

Then, a rustling sound drew his attention to the base of the old oak tree. There, illuminated by the rising moon, was his old nemesis — the armadillo. The creature was rooting around in the dirt, seemingly unconcerned with Clay's presence.

"Hey!" Clay lurched to his feet, the world tilting dangerously around him.

The armadillo looked up, meeting his gaze with what Clay would later swear was a smirk, before casually scuttling into a hole at the base of the tree.

38

Clay stumbled over, dropped to his knees and peered into the darkness. A leg trap he'd set near the entrance was still armed, waiting for its prey. "How the hell'd he get past this?" In his moonshine-addled state, Clay reached for it, fascinated and confused by the gleam of metal in the growing darkness.

"What the sam hill?" he muttered, testing the spring mechanism with unsteady fingers.

SNAP!

The trap closed on his hand with the decisive finality of karma catching up with its target. After a delayed reaction worthy of a cartoon character, Clay let out a yelp that probably startled every nocturnal creature within a mile radius.

Nursing his throbbing hand and his wounded pride, Clay staggered back to the house. He returned moments later with a flashlight and — because, clearly, he hadn't ever learned any lessons about overkill — a chainsaw.

Clay stood swaying before the oak tree, shining his flashlight down into the armadillo's burrow. "C'mon out here and fight like a man!" he bellowed, his words slurring together like a horde of kids rushing to get in line for recess.

The armadillo, unsurprisingly, declined this invitation to combat.

Undeterred, Clay fired up the chainsaw, its angry buzz shattering the peaceful night air. He attacked the tree with the unsteady determination of the thoroughly soused, sending sawdust flying in all directions. The acrid scent of sap and smoke filled his nostrils as the teeth tore deeper into the aged wood.

For a moment, Clay wavered, the chainsaw drooping in his grip as a flicker of doubt penetrated his moonshine-fortified confidence. What was he doing? What had he become? The old Clay — the one who'd played in this very yard with Maddie, who'd seen wonder instead of enemies in every creature — would never have ....

But then the moment passed, drowned in a fresh wave of bitter determination. He glared at the hole where the armadillo had disappeared, his grip tightening on the saw's handle.

"You dadjim armadilla!" he snarled. "I had it with ya!"

As if in revolt to this declaration of war, the chainsaw sputtered and died, its final revolution accompanied by a sad little cough of exhaust. Clay tried to revive it, several times, but nothin doin'. He stood there for a moment, staring at the now-silent tool as if it had personally betrayed him.

Clay then, suspecting a cause, clumsily unscrewed the gas cap and tilted the saw upward to peer into its tiny tank. Unwise, he concluded, as the last little bit of burning lava spilled into his curious eye; proving that, indeed, there was still a little bit of fuel left.

Howling in pain, Clay stumbled across his yard like a drunken sailor in a storm, arms outstretched as he made his way to the garden hose coiled against the house. After several failed attempts to locate the spigot with his one good eye, he finally managed to turn it on full blast. Clay stuck his face directly into the stream, the cold water providing blessed relief as it washed away the burning gasoline. Satisfied his eyeball wasn't actually melting, and because clearly the situation called for more poor decisions, he lurched back to the shed for a gas can.

Returning to his arboreal adversary, Clay attempted to refuel the chainsaw. In his current state, this simple task became a comedy of errors. More gas ended up on the ground than in the tank, creating a growing puddle around the base of the tree. When the can tipped over, sending fuel cascading into the armadillo's burrow, Clay's only response was an annoyed, "Comfound it!"

He righted the can with exaggerated care, then dropped to his knees to peer into the hole again. The borrowed flashlight from his shirt pocket provided only weak illumination, flickering like a lightning bug with dying batteries. No amount of banging or cursing could convince it to shine brighter.

As Clay patted down his pockets in search of inspiration, his fingers closed around his lighter. A slow grin spread across his face as he flicked it open, the small flame dancing in the darkness. He leaned forward, squinting into the hole and ....

WHOOSH!

The tree went up like a January Christmas tree, flames racing up the trunk with frightening speed. Clay stumbled backward, landing hard on his rear as tongues of fire licked hungrily at the ancient wood.

In the dancing firelight, something caught his eye — markings on the trunk that made his heart stop dead in his chest. There, carved into the bark and now illuminated by his own foolishness, were two sets of initials carved inside a jagged heart:

'C.H. + M.W.'

Clay and Maddie. A reminder of simpler times, of summer days that seemed to stretch forever, of a boy who knew how to love without fear and a girl who saw the best in him.

"No! Maddie!" The word came out as a broken whisper. Clay reached toward the burning initials, his hand recoiling from the heat.

Panic seized him as reality came crashing back. He needed to put this out. Had to stop it before the flames consumed this last precious link to his past. His wild gaze darted around the yard, finally landing on the garden hose that had recently become his eye's savior.

Clay scrambled to his feet, nearly taking a digger in his haste to reach the spigot. He cranked it on full blast, grabbed the hose, and charged toward the blaze like a drunken firefighter. The hose unfurled behind him as he ran, somehow managing not to tangle around his legs — a small blessing in a day falling well short in its quota of blessings.

But ten feet from the tree, physics and fate conspired against him. The hose reached its full length, and, thanks to Clay's iron grip on it, brought him to an abrupt and spectacular halt. His feet flew up in front of him as if he'd been yanked backward by an invisible hand, like a dog being tamed by its underestimated chain, and he crashed to the ground with a thud that seemed to rattle every bone in his body.

Above him, the flames climbed higher, sparks dancing against the night sky like malicious fireflies. Then came an ominous sound that sobered Clay faster than a bucket of ice water — the deep, wooden groan of a tree deciding to defy gravity.

With a mighty crack that seemed to split the very air, the old oak began to snap and topple. Clay watched in horror as it fell, as if in slow motion, directly toward his house. The impact shook the ground, sending up a fresh shower of sparks as the burning trunk crashed into his roof.

The flames, now finding fresh fuel in the dry timbers of his home, began to spread with terrifying speed.

What had he done?

Panic seized Clay as he watched his past and present going up in flames. He raced around the yard, coughing and sputtering as smoke filled his lungs, looking for anything that might help extinguish the growing inferno. The garden hose, still pathetically short of reaching the blaze, sprayed uselessly into the air like nature's own laugh track.

Through the smoke and chaos and the open door of his shed, his bleary eyes landed on a 5-gallon bucket sitting innocently next to his moonshine still. In that moment, pickled by his own hooch and desperate for a solution, it seemed like divine intervention.

"Sweet mercy, that's it!" he exclaimed, stumbling toward the shed.

Now, had Clay been sober, several critical thoughts might have occurred to him. He might have remembered that this particular bucket contained the high-proof "starter" batch of his prized moonshine. He might have recalled his eighth-grade science teacher's lecture about the flammability of alcohol. He might even have noticed the small 'DANGER – FLAMMABLE' label he'd stuck on the bucket himself in a rare moment of foresight.

But Clay *was not* sober. Clay was, in fact, about as far from sober as a human being could get while still maintaining vertical mobility.

Snatching the bucket with grim determination, he charged back outside. The burning tree had now fully breached his roof, creating a scene that looked like something out of a biblical plague. Smoke billowed into the night sky, and the crackle of flames provided a steady backbeat to the symphony of destruction.

Without a moment's hesitation — because hesitation might have brought with it unwelcome clarity — Clay heaved the contents of the bucket at the base of the burning tree.

Time seemed to slow.

In the fraction of a second before physics and chemistry collided in spectacular fashion, Clay had time to notice several things: the graceful arc of liquid catching the firelight, the way the flames seemed to reach eagerly toward this new offering, and the sudden, crystal-clear memory of his high school chemistry teacher saying, "Now pay attention, this part's important."

Then the world exploded. A sonic boom rang out, a blinding flash of light lit up Clay's entire neighborhood, and a miniature purple mushroom cloud blossomed from his backyard.

5 - A Blast from the Past

The current landscape surrounding Clay dissolved and was replaced by the warm, familiar contours of his childhood home. He blinked, disoriented, as a scene from his past unfolded before him.

In the living room, a younger version of himself, no more than three years old, sat at the table, a birthday cake glowing with candles. His parents beamed at him from across the table.

"What in the ...? " Clay murmured, watching his toddler self, blowing out the candles with gusto.

The scene shifted, and now Clay saw himself as a rambunctious four-year-old, rolling in the grass with a puppy. His laughter rang out, high and sweet, as the dog licked his face. His parents watched from the porch; their faces soft with affection.

"Well, look at that," Clay chuckled. "I was a handsome little devil, wasn't I?"

More memories flashed by, each one a snapshot of a different stage of Clay's youth. Five-year-old Clay, snuggled up with his mother as she read him a bedtime story. Six-year-old Clay, standing proud in his Cub Scout uniform at his swearing-in ceremony. Eight-year-old Clay, playing catch with his father in the backyard, the sun casting long shadows on the grass.

And then, nine-year-old Clay, fishing with his grandfather at the lake, their lines cast out into the peaceful, rippling water.

Clay felt a lump form in his throat as he watched these long-forgotten moments of innocence and joy. He'd been so happy then, so carefree. Before the world had sharpened its claws and teeth.

The scene changed again, and Clay found himself standing in a classroom. His middle-school teacher was addressing the students, a smile on her face.

"Good morning, class. I would like you all to meet a new classmate of ours. Come on in, Maddie."

Clay's heart skipped a beat as a young girl entered the room. She was smiling shyly, her blonde hair caught up in braids. When her eyes met Clay's, she gave him a little wink.

"Maddie," Clay breathed, reaching out a hand as if to touch her. But his fingers passed through empty air.

He watched, transfixed, as young Maddie introduced herself to the class. "My father is a biology professor at the University of Texas," she said, her voice clear and confident. "And I really like animals too."

The scene dissolved, reforming in the school hallway. Young Maddie stood before a bulletin board, studying a flyer for the 4-H club. Behind her, young Clay watched, his eyes wide with admiration.

In the next moment, Clay saw himself bursting into his living room, the 4-H brochure clutched in his hand. He bounced up and down next to his mother's recliner, waving the paper excitedly.

"Please, Ma, please?" he begged, his voice high and eager.

46

More memories rushed by, each one centered around Clay and Maddie's budding friendship:

The two of them at the 4-H competition, Maddie proudly displaying her ribbons and trophies, Clay proudly holding his 'precipitant' ribbon, as he mistakenly called it.

Playing doctor in Clay's backyard, young Maddie solemnly examining a patient feline while Clay waited attentively with popsicle stick tongue depressors.

Chasing each other by the creek, their laughter ringing out across the water. The moment when Clay, looking back to wave at Maddie, tumbled head over heels into the ravine. Maddie's gasp of fear, quickly turning to relief and giggles as she helped him up, brushing leaves from his hair.

And then, the two of them at the beach, putting the finishing touches on a lopsided sandcastle. Young Clay, seized by a sudden urge, leaping to his feet and stomping through their creation like a rampaging monster. Maddie's shock melting into laughter as she tackled him into the sand.

Their eyes meeting, their faces inches apart. Maddie leaning in, her lips brushing Clay's in a sweet, innocent kiss. His first kiss. The one he'd never forgotten.

Clay watched the sun set over the young couple's silhouette, his chest aching with a bittersweet mix of nostalgia and loss.

"Oh, Maddie," he whispered, his voice rough with emotion.

The final scene was the hardest to watch. Clay saw his younger self carving a heart into the old oak tree in his backyard, Maddie and his initials etched deep into the bark. Tears streaked the boy's face as he worked, the knife trembling in his hand.

Maddie's hand on his shoulder, turning him to face her. Her own eyes bright with unshed tears.

"We can write each other every day," she promised, her voice wavering but determined. "It's going to be OK."

Young Clay's face crumpled. "Why does your dad have to go back to New Zealand?" he asked, his voice small and lost. "Why can't you just stay here? You can stay with us."

But Maddie shook her head, her braids swinging. "Clay, I wish I could. But you know I can't do that." She held up an envelope, pressing it into his hand. "I wrote you a special letter. But you can't read it until after I leave. It has my new address and phone number. Promise me you'll write me today."

Young Clay nodded, too choked up to speak. He clung to Maddie, burying his face in her neck.

"I will," he managed finally. "As soon as I stop crying, I promise. I'll mail you a letter today."

Maddie cupped his face in her hands, kissing him one last time. And then she was gone, walking out of the yard, out of his life. Young Clay sank to his knees in the dirt, his shoulders shaking with sobs.

In his grief, he didn't notice the letter flutter from his hand, caught by a sudden breeze. Didn't see the curious baby armadillo snatch it up and scurry away into the underbrush.

"That dadjim armadilla," Clay growled as he watched the scene play out of his crushed childhood, the pieces of the puzzle now falling into place. "I shoulda knowed it was him all along."

48

He watched his younger self spin around, searching frantically for the lost letter. Glaring at his dog with unfounded suspicion, never guessing the real culprit.

The scene began to fade, the colors bleeding together like a watercolor in the rain. But before it disappeared completely, one last memory flickered to life.

Clay, now a teenager, sat slumped in the backseat of his parents' car. He was half-asleep, lulled by the motion and the soft murmur of voices from the front seat.

And then, a screech of tires. A flash of fur as something darted into the road. His father wrenching the wheel, his face a mask of panic.

The world tilting, spinning. The sickening crunch of metal and wood and stone.

And then ... darkness.

Clay came back to himself with a gasp, his heart pounding against his ribs like a snared bird. He was on his knees in the endless, white void of the heavens, tears streaming down his face.

Those memories, those precious moments, those *painful* moments ... they were all he had left of his old life. Of the person he used to be, before grief and anger had twisted him into someone unrecognizable.

Before he'd lost his way.

6 - The Pearly Gates

For a moment, Clay stood outside of Heaven with a blank, melancholy look on his face. After a moment, he focused and saw a gate with a long line of people waiting to get in.

He observed as a humble, poorly-dressed couple exited a chariot that had pulled up in front of the pearly gates. They approached the doorman standing at a podium, who asked their names, checked his list, and waved them through.

Clay watched as another woman went through a similar routine. This time, however, the doorman pointed the woman to the end of the line, much like at an exclusive nightclub with limited capacity.

"Sweet Mercy!" Clay exclaimed. "I been repo'd!"

He walked over to the gate entrance to speak with the attendant, whose name tag read 'Pete.'

"Hey, what the hell's goin' on h...." Clay started, but cut himself off when Pete shot him an offended look. "Er, uh, sorry. I mean heck."

"Your name, please, Sir?" Pete inquired calmly.

Clay laughed nervously, looking around at the others in line to see their reactions when he said, "What, you mean you don't already know?"

Pete glanced up from his clipboard, not amused and saying nothing. Somewhat ashamed, Clay cleared his throat.

"Uh, that would be Ordell Clayton Hart," he provided. Then, lowering his voice as if sharing privileged information, he added, "But you can call me Clay."

Pete scanned through the list, but found no such name. "I'm sorry, sir. You'll have to get in line."

"What? You sure about that?" Clay sputtered. "My folks are in there; I wouldn't want to worry 'em, you know how it goes."

Pete remained unmoved, standing silently.

"Look, Maître D' or Concierge or whoever you are, I'm sure we can work out some sorta deal here."

He reached for his wallet, only to find it missing. Shocked, Clay patted his pockets.

"What the ...?" Catching himself, he smiled innocently at Pete.

Clay surveyed the line. Spotting a suspicious hippie type, he narrowed his eyes. "I know it was you," he accused the man.

"Sir, please." Pete sighed, gesturing for Clay to move to the end of the queue.

Nodding politely, Clay made his way to the back of the line. Just then, an announcement came over what sounded like heaven's PA system, with a voice remarkably similar to Star Trek's computer:

"Gabriel, please report to the throne room. Gabriel to the throne room."

Clay looked around, trying to pinpoint the source of the voice. He had just taken his place in line next to a woman with a devastated expression on her face when the voice boomed out again:

52

"Your attention please, will Ordell Clayton Hart please report to the front gate. Clay to the front gate, please."

Perking up, Clay grabbed his waistband and hiked up his britches. "Well, it's about time they got their list straight!" he said to himself.

As he passed the hippie again, Clay couldn't resist a parting shot. "You're gonna get yours," he muttered. "Yes sir, you're gonna get yours!"

But when Clay reached the front, instead of Pete, an angel was waiting for him.

"Please follow me, Mr. Hart," the radiant figure instructed.

"Much obliged!" Clay started towards the pearly gates, but the angel began walking in a different direction. Pete caught Clay's arm.

"Gabriel. Follow Gabriel," he clarified, pointing.

Clay hustled to catch up to the angel, craning his head to look back longingly at the gates.

"Oh, we must be goin' to the VIP suites," he said, trying to match Gabriel's stride.

After walking a bit further, Gabriel stopped and turned to face Clay.

"What happened, Clay?" the angel asked, his voice gentle but probing.

Clay blinked, confused by the question. "Well, I reckon I blowed myself up pretty good."

"Not that," Gabriel clarified. "I mean, what happened to Clay? The sweet young boy with so much promise. What happened?"

Caught off guard, Clay stammered. "Whaddya mean?"

Gabriel held his gaze, silently demanding an honest answer. Clay shifted uncomfortably.

"I had me a rough life," he said finally. "But you oughta know that already. Ain't y'all supposed to be psychic or somethin'?"

"I know everything about you, Clay. Even more than you know about yourself. And much more than you're willing to admit."

The thought of what secrets the angel might know made Clay squirm, but he tried to play it off.

"Well, if you know everything about me, why don't you tell *me* what happened?" Clay challenged, trying to mask his unease about what secrets the angel might know.

Gabriel fixed Clay with a penetrating stare. "How about that time you went 'fishing'?"

"Fishin'? What's wrong with fishin'?" Clay spread his hands innocently. "If God didn't want us to fish, he wouldn't have created bait."

"I think you know what I'm talking about, Clay."

A flicker of recognition crossed Clay's face before he quickly masked it with feigned confusion. "Nuh ... I ...."

"Here, let me give you some help remembering that."

Clay watched in amazement as Gabriel made a gesture in midair. Using his two index fingers, the angel brought them together at a single point and spread them diagonally, zooming open a 'window' that looked like something out of a high-tech movie. Through it, Clay could see himself in an old, aluminum fishing boat.

"Hey, that's pretty nifty," Clay said, momentarily distracted from his discomfort.

Gabriel smirked. "Isn't it? Mr. Jobs helped us with that one."

With a tap of his finger, the angel set the scene in motion. Clay watched, his swagger dissolving, as his past sins played out before him.

Through the celestial window, Clay watched himself drop anchor from the aluminum fishing boat. Then he witnessed his past self holding a lit stick of dynamite, standing up in the boat with a manic grin as he held it aloft.

"Here fishy, fishy, fishy. Ha!" Past Clay called out.

Just then, a small flock of ducks landed thirty feet away. Past Clay's eyes lit up with destructive inspiration. He crouched down, trying to be sneaky – but in his enthusiasm, he failed to notice that the lit fuse had now ignited several other sticks of dynamite at his feet.

Standing back up, Past Clay hurled the stick in his hands toward the ducks. While he waited for the firework to erupt, the sizzling sound finally caught his attention. He looked down, eyes widening as he spotted the dynamite at his feet. After a moment of panicked indecision, flailing back and forth, he dove overboard.

Present Clay winced as he watched his prior self immediately sink beneath the surface, forgetting one crucial detail – he couldn't swim.

"Help! I can't swim! I can't swim!" Past Clay's gurgled screams bubbled up through the water.

Underwater, Past Clay's eyes went wide as he found himself face-to-face with several, very surprised, fish. The first stick of dynamite exploded above him, blowing a hole in the bottom of the boat. As a result, the other lit sticks now dropped through, sinking into the water all around him.

In desperation, Past Clay tried to run underwater, his limbs moving in almost comical slow-motion.

Above, the water erupted in a geyser as the sunken dynamite finally detonated.

The scene panned out to show an overhead view of the slowly flowing river. Dead fish floated into view on the surface of the water, drifting downstream, followed by Clay's own unconscious form, in a sort of parade of zombies.

The window winked shut, leaving Clay and Gabriel standing in uncomfortable silence. Clay's face had gone a telling shade of red.

"Yeah, I uh ... guess that probably wasn't the nicest thing to do, huh?" Clay mumbled, unable to meet Gabriel's eyes. After a moment, he rallied slightly. "So, what are you sayin'? Eatin' animals is bad or somethin'?"

Gabriel pinched the bridge of his nose. "Not at all. We enjoy a good venison steak up here every now and again. Why do you humans have to compartmentalize everything into extreme, definitive boxes? Can't moderation, responsibility and reason be your guide?"

Clay's brow furrowed as he tried to parse the angel's words. But Gabriel was already moving on, his expression serious once more.

"Tell me, Clay. What's the last thing you remember, right before arriving here?"

"What, you mean gettin' blowed up, or ...?"

But Gabriel was already waving his hand, the shimmering window reappearing. This time, Clay's silent pleading shake of his head told Gabriel he knew exactly what memory was coming next.

Inside the window, a new scene flickered to life. It was a rerun of teenage Clay slumped in the backseat of his parents' car, half-asleep as they drove down a dark country road. Suddenly, the dog darted into the

56

headlights. His father swerved to avoid it, sending the car careening off the road and into a large tree.

"Damn dog," Clay muttered bitterly, watching the scene unfold. "That damn dog."

The window shifted to show a stark hospital room. Teen Clay lay in a bed, his face a mask of bandages and bruises. A doctor stood over him, lips moving soundlessly as he delivered the news that would shatter Clay's world forever.

Another shift brought them to the cemetery. Teen Clay stood before two coffins, tears streaming down his face despite his attempt to maintain a hard expression. A younger Pastor Matt stood at his side, one hand resting on Clay's shoulder in silent support.

"Oh Matt," Clay's voice broke as he watched. "Pastor ... why?"

The final scene materialized in a lawyer's office. Clay, barely eighteen but already developing the emotional walls that would define his adult life, sat across from a somber-suited man.

"Are you sure, Ordell?" the lawyer asked gently. "Your aunt and uncle in Oklahoma would gladly take you in."

Teen Clay's jaw set, a muscle jumping in his cheek. "I'm eighteen, I'm an adult. I can take care of myself."

The window dissolved, leaving Clay staring into space, his eyes glistening with unshed tears.

Gabriel studied him thoughtfully. "So, you can take care of yourself, hmm? Don't need anyone else's help?"

Clay shook himself, the familiar defensive walls slamming back into place. "That damn dog," he snarled. "How could God let that happen? They were good people, my folks."

"There is a season and a time for everything," Gabriel began, his voice low and melodic. "A time to be born, and a time to die; a time to plant and a time to pluck up what is planted; a time to ...."

Clay cut him off, his temper flaring. "You expect me to be a saint after what I been through? Y'all did this to me! How can you hold me responsible for the way I act?" He jabbed an accusing finger at the angel, his face twisted in anger and pain. "And what's with quoting the Beatles at a time like this? What's that stupid song got to do with anything?"

"Actually, that was The Byrds," Gabriel corrected with a raised eyebrow. "And, truly, it wasn't even them; they borrowed that one from us."

Clay's brow furrowed in confusion. He hummed a few bars under his breath, "'mm mm ... ything, turn, dmm, dmm ...' Hmmm, I coulda swore that was the Beatles. Are you sure?"

Gabriel's expression remained serene, then he redirected the conversation. "I have an offer for you, Clay. A chance to regain what you've lost."

"Like one of them game shows where I get to pick what's behind the curtain?"

"Not even close." Gabriel's eyes sparkled with divine patience. "How would you like to have a second chance? What if we send you back to try again?"

Clay's brow furrowed. "What, like a baby? I gotta go through them diapers and all that? I don't reckon I could handle eatin' them jars of mushed peas again."

"No, it's not like that," Gabriel assured him. "We're offering to send you back now. Presently."

"Can I go back as Gerard Butler? Or maybe that rich Facebook guy?" Clay perked up at the possibility.

"Afraid not. There *is* a slight catch." Gabriel's tone turned matter-of-factly.

Clay tensed, waiting.

"If you choose this option, and it's fully your choice, we'll be sending you back as an animal."

"Come again?"

"We're going to send you back as an animal."

Clay's jaw dropped. "What, you mean? Like 'carnation? I'm gettin' 'carnated? That ain't in the bible." He paused, considering. "'Least I don't think so." His eyes narrowed with sudden suspicion. "So why me? Why do I get a second chance when all them folks is waiting in line?"

Gabriel put a compassionate arm on Clay's shoulder as they began to walk. "Well, that's a good question, Clay. I asked the big guy that same question myself. He said, deep down, underneath all that blubber and whiskers, there's a really good guy in you. You've changed over the years, Clay. You used to be so respectful of God's creation. But somewhere along the line it all 'went south', as you might put it. Your actions lately don't match your heart," he said.

"Wait, back up a bit." Clay's eyes narrowed. "He said blubber and whiskers?"

"Well, I added that part." Gabriel's lips twitched. "I'm paraphrasing."

Clay looked at the angel suspiciously. "Well, you should listen to Him. He's right. Look, I don't know many people who likes all the stuff God made more than me. Why, I was in 4-H."

"Never mind," Gabriel regained focus. "Back to the matter at hand. Make your choice – do you want this special offer?"

"What is this, an infomercial? I gotta act fast or the offer will dry up or somethin'?" Clay wiped his brow nervously. "What if I choose to decline this offer?"

"Then you go stand back in line and await your judgment."

Clay shifted uncomfortably as Gabriel continued, "He will ask you one simple question. Just one."

"Multiple choice?" Clay attempted a weak joke.

"Look, Clay, not everyone gets this opportunity. If you don't want it, no one is going to force it upon you." Gabriel's patience seemed to be wearing thin. "So, what's it going to be?"

Clay remained silent, sweat beading on his forehead as he wrestled with the decision.

"You know Clay, let's just forget it," Gabriel said at last. "Why don't you just go get back in line."

"Wait!" Clay burst out. "No. No, I reckon there's a pretty good reason I'm being given a second chance. I mean, if I was good to go, why would I need a second chance, right?"

Gabriel looked intrigued by this flash of logic. Clay nervously smacked his lips before adding, "I ... I accept."

Gabriel nodded as if he'd known this would be the answer all along. "Wise decision. Walk with me."

60

He led Clay over to a lamp stand that held a single, white, unlit candle. As Gabriel spoke, he simply looked at the candle and it ignited.

"Do you know what this is, Clay?"

Clay looked at Gabriel curiously, answering with careful consideration, not wanting to get it wrong. "A candle?"

Gabriel turned to him. "That is correct."

Clay gave a proud smile, licking his finger and stroking it in mid-air, making a gesture as if giving himself a point.

"But it's not just a candle, Clay," Gabriel continued. "This is *your* candle."

"OK, well that's mighty nice of you, Gabriel. Thank ya. It's a really nice candle." Clay looked pleased with the apparent gift.

Gabriel paused, clearly wanting Clay to grasp something deeper. "Pay attention, Clay. *This* is *your* candle."

Clay scratched his head, at a loss for how to respond. He leaned in and sniffed. "Is it one of them smelly candles? Them's nice."

Gabriel shook his head in disbelief. "This is hopeless. But, let's get on with it, shall we? Are you ready?"

"Well, I reckon I am, but ...." Clay hedged, searching for another delay. "Real quick, what exactly is my goal here? Is there a lesson I'm supposed to learn or something?"

"Clay, if I gave you all the answers then there really wouldn't be any point in giving you a chance to learn it for yourself, right?"

"Well ...." Clay fumbled for more questions, but came up empty.

"So, you're ready?" Gabriel pressed.

Clay tried desperately to think of something else to say, anything to postpone what was coming, but words failed him. He stood there, mouth opening and closing like a fish out of water.

"Good luck," Gabriel said cheerfully.

Before Clay could protest further, the angel grabbed him by the seat of his pants and the back of his collar. With a mighty heave that would have done a professional bowler proud, Gabriel launched Clay into the unknown.

As Clay tumbled through the ether, his last coherent thought was that maybe – just maybe – he should have asked a few more questions about exactly what kind of animal he was about to become.

7 - Buggin' Out

Clay suddenly popped back into existence and found himself in the wreckage of his earthly home. Everything seemed impossibly huge — walls towered like canyon cliffs; furniture loomed like mountains. The pungent smell of smoke and spilled moonshine filled his newly-heightened senses. He was somewhat surprised that anything was left un-torched on his property, but apparently Texan firefighters know their business.

"Sweet mercy," he muttered, his voice emerging as a faint chirp. "My house looks *way* bigger than I remember."

He tried to look down at himself, to figure out what kind of creature he'd become, but his new body refused to cooperate. Everything felt alien — too many legs, antennae twitching with unfamiliar sensations.

"What in tarnation am I anyway?" he wondered aloud, scuttling awkwardly across the debris-strewn floor. A gleam of light beneath the back door caught his attention. "Well, might as well see where that leads."

As he picked his way through the wreckage, Clay passed near a puddle of his homemade moonshine, leaking out of a bottle from his previous batch. He caught a glimpse of his reflection in the liquid and froze.

"I'm a dadjim cockroach?" The horror of realization hit him like a physical blow. "Of all the no-good, dirty-dealing ...."

The moonshine's aroma was too tempting to resist, though, and distracted him from his complaints. Clay scampered over, his many legs working with unsettling coordination, and lowered his head to the small puddle saturating the carpet.

The first sip burned like hellfire, searing down what passed for a cockroach gullet. But dadjim if it didn't taste like sweet nectar. He gulped down a few more mouthfuls, relishing the familiar burn.

A belch worked its way up his throat, emerging as a high-pitched chirp that startled him. "Sweet mercy!" He shook his head, trying to clear it as the alcohol hit his significantly reduced bloodstream. "Reckon my tolerance ain't what it used to be."

The journey to the door was an obstacle course of epic proportions. Clay scurried under fallen beams, leaped over piles of debris, and skirted around precariously balanced chunks of roof. The world swayed slightly, whether from his new perspective or the moonshine, he couldn't rightly say.

Finally, he reached a small platform just below the tantalizing strip of daylight. Clay paused to catch his breath, his tiny lungs heaving with exertion. Just a few more inches, just gotta get over the top of that funny looking lever, and he'd be outside. He gathered himself, ready to make one final leap, and ....

WHAM!

Out of nowhere, a cinder block dropped from above, turning Clay's insect body into purée.

When Clay came to, he was lying face down; spread-eagle. Gabriel loomed over him, a stopwatch in one hand and a clipboard in the other.

"Ah! We have a new record," the angel announced, clicking the stopwatch with a satisfied nod.

Clay groaned, trying to move his previously flattened body. Every inch of him felt like it had been steamrolled by a freight train. Gabriel made the stopwatch and clipboard vanish with a flick of his wrist, crouching down to peer at Clay with a mixture of amusement and curiosity.

"So tell me, Clay. What did you learn?"

It took Clay a moment to find his voice. When he did, it emerged as a pitiful croak. "Well, I learned my mousetrap invention works on cockroaches too."

Gabriel chuckled, shaking his head. Clay managed to sit up, wincing at the chorus of aches and pains that flared through his battered body.

"Now I know how all them cartoon characters feel when they get smushed by a one-ton ACME anvil," he grumbled.

His gaze fell on the candle, still burning merrily away on its stand. The wax had melted down slightly shorter, the flame guttering in a pool of its own making.

"Yep, still burning," Gabriel confirmed, following Clay's gaze. He clapped a hand on Clay's back, nearly sending him sprawling again. Clay looked up at the angel, a questioning look on his face. He was starting to get the sense that the candle represented something important, but he couldn't quite put his finger on what.

Gabriel seemed to read his thoughts. "Perhaps we should start you off a little higher up in the food chain, yes?"

Before Clay could respond, the angel grabbed him by the collar and the seat of his pants, hoisting him aloft like a scruffed kitten.

"Wait!" Clay yelped, flailing his limbs in a panic. "Ain't there supposed to be a mission or something? I'm not asking you to spell it out for me, but throw me a bone here! What's the dang point of all this? Can I buy a vowel or something?"

Gabriel sighed, setting Clay back down. "Okay, let's chat for a minute. Think back, Clay. When would you say the change in you really started? The moment it all began to go sideways?"

Clay pondered the question, his brow furrowing in concentration. After a long moment, he looked up, a glimmer of realization in his eyes.

"Before my parents died ... it was Maddie. When Maddie left. That was the first terrible thing I can remember happening to me. I lost the letter she gave me, and her address along with it. She never wrote to me again after that."

A pang of old hurt flashed across Clay's face. "Why didn't she write to me?" he asked softly, almost to himself.

Gabriel gave him a patient look. "Probably because you never wrote to her."

Clay's head snapped up, a mix of emotions playing out on his face. Astonishment, hurt, skepticism.

"But I lost the letter!" he protested. "My dog ate it! Well, actually, it was that dadjim armadilla's fault come to find out. I promised Maddie I'd write, but I couldn't. Y'all took that chance away from me. And you took *Maddie herself* away from me. How is that fair?"

Gabriel shrugged, unmoved by Clay's outburst. "Based on *your* understanding of fairness? It's not."

Clay opened his mouth to argue, but Gabriel wasn't finished.

"Tell me something, Clay - don't you think it's a bit self-centered to assume we took *her* away from *you*? Ever consider that maybe we took *you* away from *her*? For *her* protection?"

The words stung Clay. His mouth hung open, any protest dying in his throat. The thought that maybe - just maybe - Maddie *had* been spared from witnessing the man he would eventually become.

As much as he hated to admit it, Gabriel probably had a point. After all, he reckoned, an angel likely had a few more smarts than he did.

"What did it say?" he asked finally, his voice weak with humility. "The letter, I mean. What was in it?"

Gabriel smiled, a faraway look in his eyes. "Ah, the brilliance of a child. Maddie had more life, more wisdom in that one letter than most folks manage in a lifetime. And she was just a kid."

Clay felt a pang of shame twist in his gut. He'd always known Maddie was special. That she saw things, understood things in a way he never could. But to hear it spelled out so plainly ....

"She has what you lack," Gabriel continued, his voice gentle but firm. "Discover the spirit of her letter, Clay. Let it sink into your bones, bury itself in your heart. Only then will you find the healing you seek."

A flicker of hope ignited in Clay's chest. But it was quickly doused by a wave of confusion.

"But how?" he asked, throwing up his hands. "How am I supposed to find the 'spirit' of a letter I ain't even got? Heck, I don't even know if the dang thing still exists! Knowing my luck, it probably rotted years ago."

Gabriel held up a hand, cutting off Clay's frustrated tirade.

"Actually, the letter does still exist. But you're missing the point, son. It's not about the physical object. It's about the essence of Maddie's words. The love and light she poured onto that paper."

Clay shook his head, still not quite grasping the concept.

"Look at it this way," Gabriel tried again. "What do you think your life would have been like if you'd never lost that letter? If you'd stayed connected to Maddie all these years?"

A shadow of regret passed over Clay's face. He'd be lying if he said he'd never wondered the same thing himself, on those long, lonely nights when the weight of his mistakes pressed down like a physical thing.

"Well, for starters, I didn't lose it," he said softly. "Not really. If y'all hadn't let that armadilla steal it away, I wouldn't have broken my promise to Maddie. I would've written to her, kept her in my life. And who knows? Maybe things would've turned out different. Maybe I wouldn't of ...."

He trailed off, unable to finish the thought. But Gabriel nodded, understanding shining in his eyes.

"Perhaps," the angel allowed. "Her friendship certainly couldn't have hurt. But son, do you really believe one little letter is solely responsible for the man you became? For the choices you made?"

Clay opened his mouth, ready to argue. But something in Gabriel's gaze stopped him. A glimmer of hard-won wisdom, of a truth Clay had been running from for far too long.

He deflated, his shoulders slumping. "I ... I don't know," he admitted finally. "I guess not. It's just ... it's easier, you know? To blame it on something, someone else. Because if it's all on me ...."

68

Gabriel laid a gentle hand on Clay's shoulder. "I know, son. Believe me, I know. But that's the funny thing about free will. It's both a blessing and a burden. The power to choose...and the responsibility that comes with it."

Clay sighed, rubbing a hand over his face. He suddenly felt very tired...and very, very small.

"So, what now?" he asked, a note of defeat in his voice. "I don't suppose we could just get on with, well, whatever this is? Send me back, let me take my lumps and be done with it?"

But Gabriel was already shaking his head. "Not quite, I'm afraid. You've got quite a long way to go before you reach the level of understanding you lack."

The angel made a shooing motion, urging Clay to turn around. With a heavy sigh, Clay complied, bracing himself for what he knew was coming.

"Alrighty then," he muttered, sticking his rear end out and squeezing his eyes shut. "Let 'er rip."

He heard Gabriel chuckle behind him. Felt the angel's hands grasp him firmly by the collar and the seat of his pants.

And then, with a mighty heave, Clay was airborne once more, hurtling into the unknown.

As he tumbled head over heels through the ether, a single thought crystallized in Clay's mind.

If this was the Almighty's idea of a joke, he sure as heck wasn't laughing.

8 - A Bird's Eye View

Like a miniature starship returning from a hyperspace jump, Clay suddenly appeared in the sky, hurtling through the air with his wings flapping frantically of their own accord. He let out a startled quack as he tried to get his bearings, loose feathers trailing in his wake.

"Sweet Mercy," he muttered to himself, his voice emerging as a series of irritated quacks. "I'm a dadjim duck!"

Clay managed a somewhat clumsy landing onto a metro sidewalk, waddling along the local storefronts until he caught his reflection in one of the display windows. He shook his head in disbelief, still trying to process his latest transformation.

At an intersection, Clay instinctively stopped, waiting for the walk signal to change. The people waiting at the crosswalk gawked at the sight of a duck obeying traffic laws.

When the sign displayed an orange pedestrian, Clay started across the road. Halfway through his traverse, a speeding truck blared its horns and swerved directly toward him. With a panicked flurry of feathers, Clay scrambled to safety, his heart pounding like a jackhammer.

"Sweet Mercy!" he panted, collapsing against a wall to catch his breath. "Ya almost hit me, ya maniac!"

As the adrenaline wore off, Clay glanced at his wings thoughtfully, giving them an experimental flap.

"Hey, hold the boat. Why am I walkin' when I got these?"

With a determined gleam in his eye, Clay took off running down the sidewalk, his wings pumping furiously. Slowly, miraculously, he began to lift off the ground.

"Woohoo!" he cried, his voice lost to the wind. "Now this is more like it!"

But Clay's triumph was short-lived. His flight path was erratic, sending him careening off lampposts and building facades like a feathered pinball. It took every ounce of concentration just to stay airborne.

Gradually, though, he got the hang of it. Soon he was soaring above the Texas countryside, the wind ruffling his feathers as he executed wobbly loops and turns.

"Here I go, into the wild blue yonder," he sang tunelessly, his duck voice warbling on the high notes. "Da da daaa, da da da daaaa."

Up ahead, a glimmer of water caught Clay's eye. With a banking turn, he aimed himself at the wetland, visions of a graceful water landing playing in his head.

What he got, instead, was a crash course in gravity. Clay hit the surface of the pond like a skipping stone, leaving a trail of impressive splashes before pile-driving beak-first into a cluster of cattails.

"Ugh," he groaned, dragging himself up onto the shore. "I really gotta work on my landings."

As he paddled out into the tranquil water, Clay couldn't help but marvel at the novelty of it all. Here he was, bobbing along like a living bath toy, not a care in the world. It was almost enough to make him forget his predicament.

Almost.

"So, what now?" he asked the empty air, his duck voice small and lost. "What am I supposed to do?"

As if on cue, a familiar voice sounded in his head.

"Find that which you have lost."

Clay nearly leapt out of his feathers. He spun around, scanning the sky for the source of the voice.

"Gabriel? That you? Where ya hidin'?"

A ripple in the water drew his attention downward. There, floating serenely beside him, was a green frog. A very familiar green frog.

"I'm not hiding, Clay," Frog Gabriel said patiently. "I'm right here."

Clay goggled at the amphibious angel, his bill hanging open in astonishment. "What the heck are you doin' here? And why are you a frog, of all things?"

Gabriel shrugged, a curiously human gesture for a frog. "Just checking in," he said, his bulbous eyes blinking slowly. "Seeing how you're adjusting to your new form."

Clay let out a derisive quack. "How do you think I'm doin'? I'm a duck, for cryin' out loud! I can't talk, I ain't got no thumbs; how am I supposed to figure anything out like this?"

The frog regarded him calmly, unperturbed by the outburst. "Well, I suppose we have to start somewh ...."

Gabriel broke off, his gaze drawn to something over Clay's shoulder. Clay turned to look, spotting a cluster of fellow ducks bobbing on the water's surface.

"Oops, gotta run," Gabriel said hurriedly. "We'll talk later, Clay. Remember, find what you've lost!"

With a cryptic wink, the divine amphibian vanished beneath the surface, leaving only ripples in his wake.

"Hey, wait!" Clay cried, paddling frantically in circles. "Come back here and explain yourself, ya green-faced son of a ...."

But Gabriel was gone. With a huff of frustration, Clay glided over to his clan, still not knowing they were actually decoys, and settled in among their ranks.

"Well ain't this just ducky," he grumbled, eyeing his silent companions. "Hey there, fellas. Nice weather we're havin', huh?"

The decoys, of course, didn't reply. Clay wasn't sure if that made him feel better or worse.

"What's a matter?" he needled, bobbing closer to the nearest fake. "Catfish got your tongue?"

Up close, the truth became obvious. Clay let out a groan, slapping a wing over his face.

"Of course. Y'all are just hunks of painted plastic. And here I am, talkin' to ya like a dang fool."

The sudden blast of a duck call nearly sent Clay rocketing out of the water. He whipped around, catching sight of a camouflaged hunter crouched among the cattails.

"Aw, crap," he muttered, forcing his racing heart to slow. "Okay, Clay, just play it cool."

Pasting on his best inane smile, Clay froze in place, doing his darnedest to mimic the blank stares of the decoys around him. But the hunter wasn't buying it. Raising a pair of binoculars, the man scrutinized Clay with unnerving intensity.

"I'm just a decoy," Clay chanted under his breath, fighting the urge to bolt. "Just a harmless little decoy, floatin' along without a care in the world."

Slowly, inch by painstaking inch, he began to drift away from the others, still wearing that vacant grin.

Below the surface, however, his webbed feet churned furiously, propelling him away from danger with all the subtlety of an outboard motor.

The ruse might have worked, if not for the hunter's keen eye. Lowering his binoculars, the man reached for his shotgun with deliberate calm.

Clay's heart leapt into his throat. He could already picture his epitaph: 'Here lies Clay: A fowl-mouthed wise-quacker.'

But even as the hunter took aim, a dark shape streaked through the water beneath Clay's paddling feet. With a yelp of surprise, he found himself violently sucked under, a split second before the shotgun boomed overhead.

In the murky depths of the lake, Clay came face-to-face with his unlikely savior ... and screamed.

The giant catfish that had grabbed him was the stuff of nightmares — a whiskered leviathan with a gaping mouth full of Velcro teeth. Clay thrashed and flailed; his panicked quacks muffled by the water.

"It's Jaws!" he gurgled, kicking wildly at the beast. "Jaws with whiskers!"

But the monster fish was not so easily deterred. It lunged for him again, its jaws snapping shut a hair's breadth from Clay's tail feathers.

Somehow, through a combination of luck and sheer desperation, Clay managed to wriggle free of the catfish's grip. With a mighty kick of his webbed feet, he rocketed to the surface, exploding from the water in a geyser of foam.

Coughing and sputtering, he made a beeline for the shore, his wings pumping like pistons. He dove into the first burrow he saw, collapsing in a panting heap on the cool, dark earth.

But his relief was short-lived. From the depths of the tunnel came a low, menacing growl.

Clay's eyes went wide. His feathers stood on end. He opened his bill to scream ...

... and shot out of the burrow like a cork from a bottle, a plume of dirt and loose plumage billowing in his wake.

"Dadjimmit, Gabriel!" he hollered as he wheeled into the sky. "You got a sick sense of humor, ya know that?"

But even as the words left his beak, a familiar sight caught his eye in the far distance. Standing out from the patchwork of fields and fences was a small dark dot — the charred remains of a very familiar house.

"Hey, that's my place!" Clay exclaimed, angling his wings to maneuver around for a better look. "Looks a heckuva lot smaller from up here."

When he approached closer, he spotted a tiny figure standing on the sidewalk, staring at the ruined house with an unreadable expression. A jolt of recognition shot through him.

"Pastor Matt?"

Curiosity overwhelming caution, Clay circled lower, aiming for the front yard. At the last second, he remembered one crucial detail.

"Aw, dang, I don't know how to land this thing!"

With a panicked cry of "Mayday! Mayday!", Clay plowed into the grass, bouncing and skidding before coming to a decidedly ungraceful stop.

Wheezing, Clay dragged himself upright … and found himself staring into the astonished face of Pastor Matt.

"Pastor!" he cried, waddling forward eagerly. "Boy, am I glad to see you! It's me, Clay! Your old buddy from next door!"

But of course, to the pastor's ears, it all came out as a series of increasingly agitated quacks. The man took a step back, eyeing Clay like one might eye a potentially rabid animal.

Clay was so focused on trying to communicate, he almost didn't notice the car pulling up to the curb behind them. When he turned towards the sounds, a figure stepped out … and the entire world seemed to grind to a halt.

"Well, hellooooo there, gorgeous," Clay breathed, his bill falling open as he took in the vision before him. "Who is *that* absolute dish?"

The woman was breathtaking — flowing hair and soft curves, with a face that could make even a eunuch intrigued. She approached Pastor Matt with a hesitant smile, oblivious to the slack-jawed duck gawking at her from the lawn.

As she drew closer, a flicker of recognition sparked in the depths of Clay's memory. He knew that smile; knew it like he knew his own freckles.

"Maddie?" he whispered, hardly daring to believe it. "Is that really you?"

But before he could process this stunning revelation, a sound from next door shattered the moment.

"Sampson! No!" Pastor Matt's shout pierced the air as his rottweiler lunged toward Clay from the mindlessly left-open fence gate.

Clay spun around just in time to see Pastor Matt's dog come barreling towards him, a hundred-plus pounds of furry fury.

With a panicked flap of wings, Clay took to the sky, his heart hammering against his downy chest. He banked in a wide circle, watching as Pastor Matt wrestled Sampson back under control, one hand firmly gripping the dog's collar while he ushered Maddie inside with the other.

"Maddie!" Clay called out uselessly, his voice emerging as a desperate quack. He watched helplessly as she disappeared into the house, her perfume lingering on the breeze like a bittersweet memory.

Now that Sampson was safely contained, Clay attempted another landing. It was less of a touchdown and more of a controlled crash, sending him tumbling head over tail across the lawn. Shaking off his dizziness, he waddled over to Pastor Matt's house and managed to flutter up onto a convenient bush beneath an open window.

Inside, Pastor Matt's wife was playing hostess, passing Maddie a steaming cup of coffee. Clay's breath seized in his throat as he watched Maddie wrap her elegant fingers around the mug, a gesture so achingly familiar it made his heart hurt. She'd always had a way of making even the simplest movements seem graceful.

"Yeah, I think I remember you vaguely," Maddie was saying, her voice carrying that slightly musical, New Zealand lilt that Clay remembered so well. "You've always been Clay's neighbor, right?"

Pastor Matt gestured across the street. "I grew up over there, actually. It's a bit foggy, but I think I remember you too. You used to come over to Clay's and play in his backyard, right?"

A smile bloomed across Maddie's face, transforming her from merely beautiful to radiant. "Yes," she said softly, her eyes peeking out the window to the yard next door. "Yes, we did. We set up our novice animal clinic right over there," she glowed, pointing. "He turned out to be my childhood sweetheart."

"Oh, my Sweetie," Clay whispered to himself outside the other window, his soul raw with emotion.

"And funny," Maddie continued, a laugh bubbling up from somewhere deep inside her. "Oh my gosh, he was so funny! He could always make me laugh, even when I was having the worst day."

Her eyes sparkled with remembered joy. "There was this one time ... he got it in his head to build us a clubhouse. Wouldn't let anyone help him, said he was going to do it all by himself. Well, apparently his carpentry skills weren't quite what he thought they were."

She dissolved into giggles, and Clay felt his face grow warm beneath his feathers as he remembered exactly where this story was going.

"He was inside the shack, proudly showing off his handiwork, when the whole thing just ... collapsed! Just came right down on top of him. I was terrified at first, but then he stands up in the middle of all this rubble, covered in sawdust, and says, cool as a cucumber, 'Maybe we can just have a picnic on some soft blankets instead.'"

The kitchen filled with laughter, but Clay noticed something else in Maddie's eyes — a softness, a tenderness that made his heart ache.

"That was the Clay I like to remember too," Pastor Matt said warmly. "He was a good kid."

But then Pastor Matt's smile faded slightly, and Maddie caught it immediately in the way he spoke. Her own expression sobered.

"How you *like to* remember him?" she asked, leaning forward slightly.

Pastor Matt sighed, choosing his words carefully. "Sometimes things happen in a person's life and it changes them. Life can be hard on a person."

Maddie's eyes pleaded for more information, and Clay found himself holding his breath, dreading what might come out next.

"Look," Pastor Matt continued gently, "don't get me wrong. Clay is a good guy. I grew up with him too. I know who he is on the inside." He paused, his expression troubled. "It's just that after his parents passed, he sort of ... sank down into himself. He seemed to have a hard time after that letting his heart come through."

Maddie's brow furrowed, not quite understanding. Clay could see her trying to reconcile the boy she'd known with the man Pastor Matt was now describing.

"For example," Pastor Matt offered. "His job. Clay is a 'varmint control specialist,' as he puts it. And deep down, his intentions are good. He genuinely wants to protect people from situations where nature and humanity clash. The problem is ...." He hesitated, searching for the right words. "Sometimes he might go too far. A bit too far. I wouldn't necessarily say he's cruel; just ... ambitious."

Clay watched as understanding dawned in Maddie's eyes, followed by something that looked dangerously like disappointment. It cut him to the quick, seeing that look on her face. She'd always believed in him, had seen the best in him even when he couldn't see it in himself. And now ....

Just then, Pastor Matt noticed the strange duck peering through the window. He excused himself from the table and walked over, gently shooing Clay away with a wave of his hands.

Clay heeded the Pastor's dismissal, but his mind was still fixed on Maddie's expression. She'd looked so sad, so disappointed — not angry, which somehow made it worse. It was as if she was mourning the boy she'd known, the man he could have been.

The man he still could be, maybe. If only he could figure out what Gabriel was trying to teach him.

With a heavy heart, Clay waddled into the backyard of his ruined house and plopped down in the grass. As he sat dwelling on and trying to compartmentalize the feelings he was experiencing, he saw it — the old oak tree. Even charred and broken, its trunk still stood firm — a monument to a simpler time.

He waddled over for a closer look.

Clay's gaze fell on the blackened carving near the base:

'C.H. + M.W.'

Clay and Maddie. Forever young, forever in love.

"Maddie," he sighed, running a wingtip over the scorched letters. "Look what I've done. What a mess I've made of everything."

Then, out of the corner of his eye, he spotted the armadillo hole below. Clay crouched down, sticking his head into the gloom.

"It's your fault!" he bellowed, his voice echoing in the confined space. "You hear me, you dadjim armadilla? This whole thing ... it's on you!"

But the armadillo, of course, was long gone. Probably high-tailing it for the next county, Clay thought bitterly.

He was about to pull back, to admit defeat, when a flash of red caught his eye. There, half-buried in the rubble of the hole, was a familiar toy car. The same one he'd pined after for weeks as a boy, before it vanished into the void of lost things.

Stunned, Clay reached out with his bill, snagging the little vehicle and dragging it into the light. It was scuffed and dented, the paint peeling, but unmistakably his.

"Well, I'll be," he murmured, a flood of memories washing over him. "I always wondered what happened to this little guy."

And then, glinting in the depths of the burrow, he saw something else. Something that made his heart stutter in his chest.

An envelope, yellowed with age and slightly charred at the edges but, amazingly, intact.

With a strangled cry, Clay lunged for the letter, snatching it up in his beak and stumbling backwards out of the hole.

"Maddie's letter!" he gasped, hardly daring to believe it. "After all this time!"

But his elation was short-lived. From the yard next door came the sound of frenzied barking, followed by the ominous creaking of straining wood.

Clay turned just in time to see Sampson come flying over the picket fence like a furry pumpkin in a punkin chunkin contest, grass clippings flying in his wake.

"Aw, heck," Clay groaned, eyeing the escape routes around him. He determined the fallen tree branch encroaching his roof was his most readily option, but Sampson was closing fast.

With the dog hot on his tail, Clay made a break for it, half-flapping, half-climbing his way up the limb, he tumbled onto the shingles just as Sampson's jaws snapped shut a millimeter from his rear end.

"Not today, Cujo!" Clay called down, his heart hammering against his ribs. "Maybe next time, chump!"

But his triumph was short-lived. The precious cargo clamped in his beak reminded him of the task at hand. This was it. The moment of truth.

But as he reached out to tear the seal, a sickening realization washed over him. He had no hands. No fingers.

Just a pair of useless, feathered stumps where his arms used to be.

"Dadjimmit," he groaned, glaring at his wings in betrayal. "How the heck am I supposed to open this thing?"

He tried everything — pecking at it with his bill, scraping at it with his webbed feet, even attempting to tear it open with his teeth. But the letter remained stubbornly sealed, mocking him with its secrets.

In desperation, Clay dragged the envelope to the jagged edge of a fallen branch. If he could just snag a corner, maybe he could ... but the makeshift letter-opener had other ideas.

Then, with a gust of wind, the envelope slipped from his grasp, fluttering down into the depths of his house through a crack in the roof.

"No!" Clay cried, scrambling to the edge of the hole. There it lay on his bedroom floor, tantalizingly out of reach. After everything he'd been through, after coming so close.

The door. The door had been blown off its hinges. Maybe, Clay thought, maybe hope wasn't lost after all.

Clay fluttered from the roof and squeezed himself through the back door. But dread, once again, settled in as the fallen beams and debris proved too much for his duck form. There was no way to retrieve the letter from the wreckage.

As he emerged back outside, a sense of foreboding slowly flooded over him. He hadn't thought that Sampson might still be lurking.

Surely enough, panning to his right, he found himself face-to-face, or more accurately, bill-to-canines with his nemesis.

"Oh, shiii ..."

When Clay came to, he was staring up at a familiar face. Gabriel loomed over him, a look of exasperated amusement playing across his features.

" ... iii ..." Clay exclaimed, continuing his previous cry from earth. But then his eyes bugged-out and he adjusted to a more heaven-appropriate conclusion, " ... iioooot!"

"Well, well, well," the angel drawled, shaking his head. "Look what the cat dragged in. Or should I say ... dog?"

Clay just groaned, leveling a weary glare at his celestial tormentor. Back in Heaven again, human again, and still no closer to reading that letter.

Some days, you just couldn't catch a break.

84

Clay rolled to his feet, "Aw, c'mon. Don't you think you're laying it on a bit thick with the whole karmic justice thing?"

Gabriel just smiled, patting Clay on the back. "You know what they say about karma ... it's a real beast."

Clay huffed, gingerly contorting his body. He felt like he'd been processed through a meat grinder. It hurt like the dickens, but he'd be fine.

Probably.

"So what now?" he asked, refusing to meet Gabriel's eyes. "You gonna send me back again? Turn me into a dung beetle or something?"

The angel patted Clay on the back, a tone of something almost like sympathy in his voice. "Oh, Clay. Always so quick to assume the worst." He put his hands on Clay's shoulders, squaring him compassionately. "Haven't you figured it out yet? This isn't about punishment. It's about growth. About learning to see the world through different eyes."

Clay just stared at him, uncomprehending. Gabriel sighed.

"Think about it," he pressed, tapping a finger against Clay's chest. "In the short time you were a duck, what did you experience? Fear, sure. Frustration, absolutely. But also wonder. Joy. The simple pleasure of the wind beneath your wings."

Clay thought back to his first clumsy flight, the rush of exhilaration as he soared above the treetops, the peace of floating on the tranquil pond, the warmth of the sun on his back.

"Hey, being a duck ain't all it's quacked-up ... cracked-up to be. I mean, the flying thing was actually pretty cool, I guess, but that landing part? That sucks!"

Gabriel nodded, a smile playing at the corners of his mouth. He motioned for Clay to follow as he walked toward the candle.

"Every creature, no matter how small or seemingly insignificant, has a place in the grand tapestry of life. A purpose, a unique perspective to offer."

He patted Clay on the back again, then faced him squarely. "Your problem, Clay, is that you've been so focused on your own pain, your own wants and needs, that you've lost sight of that truth. You've closed yourself off from the world, from the beauty and meaning that's all around you."

Clay hung his head, shame burning in his chest. He knew the angel was right. He'd been so consumed by his own misery, his own selfish desires, that he'd forgotten how to really live; how to love.

Standing before his celestial guide, Clay's mind still reeled from his experiences as a duck. Gabriel, ever the enigmatic mentor, turned his attention to the candle that represented Clay's mortal existence. It was noticeably shorter now, the wax melting away like sand through an hourglass.

"Yep, that sure is a nice candle," Clay remarked, trying to lighten the mood.

Gabriel glanced over, a flicker of amusement in his ancient eyes. "It sure is, Clay. Too bad it won't last forever."

"Yeah, I been wondering about that. I know you said this is my candle, but I think I might be missing some puzzle pieces here," Clay responded. "Like, what happens when it runs out? Then what? That mean my time's up or somethin'? That I'm outta chances and stuff?"

"What do you think?"

86

Clay pondered, growing more nervous. "Well, I think we're probably gonna need a much bigger candle if that's the case. Maybe a whole case of 'em."

"Maybe a whole warehouse of them," the angel predicted, grasping his hands comfortably behind his back.

"So, what's next?" Clay asked, scratching his head. "I guess I'm not done yet? How many last chances does a guy get? And please, I don't want to go back as an animal again. Just give me one more shot as myself. I gotta get back to Maddie, even if it's just to explain why I never wrote. Can't you do that for me? Please?"

Gabriel's expression softened, a glimmer of understanding in his ancient eyes. "With God, all things are possible. But what good would it do? You've proven who you are time and time again."

Clay felt a flare of defensiveness, but it quickly faded, replaced by a bone-deep weariness. "When you've lost everything, you start to think different about stuff."

The angel nodded, a hint of approval in his gaze. "I'll make you a deal, Clay. You try to figure out this thing called life, and if you show promise, I'll talk to the Big Guy, see what he's willing to do."

A spark of hope ignited in Clay's chest, fragile but undeniable. "I'll do anything. Anything."

"I don't need you to do *anything*," Gabriel countered, his voice firm. "I need you to *learn something*!"

They walked even closer to the candle, watching as the flame danced ever lower. Clay's mind raced, grasping for some shred of understanding, some key to the cosmic riddle he found himself trapped in.

"What's the deal with that dadjim armadilla?" he blurted out, frustration bleeding into his words. "Is he Satan incarnate or somethin'? How am I supposed to learn anything when he keeps jackin' up my world?"

Gabriel cocked his head, a hint of amusement playing at the corners of his mouth. "What do you mean?"

"What do I mean? He's always screwin' with me! Stealing my stuff, knowing full well I want it back. It's like he gets off on it or something."

The angel was silent for a moment, considering. Then, slowly, a look of realization dawned on his face. "He takes what isn't his, consumes more than he needs, and doesn't consider others in the process. That is a shame, Clay. Good thing you're not like that, right?"

The words hit Clay like a sucker punch to the gut. Suddenly, the armadillo's antics didn't seem so different from his own selfish behavior over the years. The realization left a bitter taste in his mouth.

He glanced at the candle, alarmed to see that it was now half its original size. "Uh, looks like we better get another candle. That one's getting shorter!"

But Gabriel just shook his head, a hint of sadness in his eyes. "There is but one."

Clay felt a surge of desperation, his mind casting about for some lifeline, some trump card to play. "Look, my neighbor was a pastor. Don't make me go over your head with this."

"Ah yes, Pastor Matt," Gabriel mused. "Your only friend, as I recall. If it wasn't for his incredible compassion and patience, you would've had no one at all."

Gabriel laid a gentle hand on Clay's shoulder. "Tell me, what do you think would happen if I sent you back as something small? Something that has to rely on wit rather than strength?"

Clay's brow furrowed. "Like what?"

A mischievous glint entered Gabriel's eyes. "Oh, I don't know ... perhaps something that knows what it's like to be hunted. To be on the other side of those traps you're so fond of setting."

Concern dawned on Clay's face. "Oh no. No, no, no ...."

"Oh yes," Gabriel said cheerfully. And before Clay could protest further, the angel gave him a mighty shove into the ethereal void.

As Clay tumbled through space and time, his form shifting and shrinking, his last coherent thought was that maybe, just *maybe*, he should have been more careful what he wished for.

9 - A Small World

Clay dropped with a plop in the middle of a suburban Texas night, finding himself now nestled among several sleeping fluffballs in what seemed to be a spacious plexiglass cage. As consciousness seeped back, he noticed everything around him seemed impossibly large — the water bottle hanging from the cage wall loomed like a community water tower, while the exercise wheel looked like a giant Ferris wheel, casting long shadows in the dimly lit pet shop.

Clay twitched a couple of times; his tiny heart racing as unfamiliar sensations flooded his senses. The smells were overwhelming — wood shavings, other animals, the lingering scent of cleaning supplies. His whiskers trembled with each new stimulus.

"Sweet mercy," he muttered to himself, his voice emerging as a series of soft squeaks. He looked down at his tiny hands, then twisted around to examine his body, nearly toppling over as he tried to process his new form. Across the cage, he could see other gerbils going about their business — some sleeping, others munching on food pellets, while a few scampered aimlessly about their enclosure.

With growing horror, Clay touched his face, then grabbed the fur on top of his head, looking upward as if seeking divine intervention. "Nooooo!" The cry of dismay echoed only in his mind as his new vocal cords produced nothing but a high-pitched squeak that barely disturbed his cage mates.

Later that morning, Clay sat motionless in the corner of the cage, boredom and indignity etched on his furry features. A few customers passed by, barely sparing a glance at the rodents on display. He watched his fellow gerbils with a mixture of fascination and disgust. One gerbil was contentedly sniffing the rear end of another, causing Clay's whiskers to twitch with revulsion.

"Ya sick bastard!" he thought, shaking his head at the display. Before he could properly express his disapproval, another gerbil approached him from behind, clearly intent on giving Clay the same treatment. He jumped to all fours, whirling to face the offender with as much dignity as his diminutive form could muster.

"Buddy, you better stop buyin' whoop-ass tickets, 'cause you're fixin' to win the lottery!" The threat came out as nothing more than an aggressive squeak, but it seemed to do the trick. The other gerbil backed off, apparently deciding this particular newcomer wasn't worth the trouble.

Satisfied with his small victory, Clay turned his attention to a gerbil enthusiastically running on a plastic wheel. He cocked his head, perplexed by the pointless activity. "Where ya think yer going, feller? Are you a moron or somethin'?"

At Clay's squeaked commentary, the gerbil hopped off the wheel. Curiosity getting the better of him, Clay climbed into it himself, walking at a leisurely pace. "Seems kinda pointless to me," he mused. But as he picked up speed, a familiar grin spread across his furry face. "Hmmm, ha! Kinda fun!"

Moments later, Clay was tearing around the wheel at top speed, the world blurring around him as he gave in to the simple joy of movement. "Wheeeeeee!" he cried, forgetting for a moment the indignity of his situation.

His revelry was cut short by an unexpected sight. A massive boa constrictor loomed outside the cage; its unblinking eyes fixed on Clay with predatory intensity. He froze, the sudden stop sending him flying out of the wheel. He landed with a thump, finding himself nose to nose with the serpent through the glass.

Two men stood on the other side — the boa's owners, Clay realized with a gulp.

"Doesn't he look delicious, Crusher?" one said, eyeing Clay hungrily.

The other man rolled his eyes. "C'mon, man. The mice are cheaper."

"I just thought we'd give him a special treat, is all."

With a smack to his friend's shoulder, the second man led him away.

Clay squeaked a sigh of relief. Then, to his amazement, he recognized another shopper strolling down his aisle. It was Maddie!

Immediately, he began scratching on the glass, like a dog wanting inside the house when it's ten below outside. "Maddie! Maddie! Over here! Save me!"

Maddie couldn't help but notice Clay's shenanigans and approached, placing a finger on the glass; a delighted smile on her face. "Oh, isn't he cute? Hi, lil' cutie!"

Clay preened at the attention, hopping around and showing off his best moves — one-armed pushups, backflips, anything to impress her. "Maddie, it's me, Clay!" he cried, desperate to make her understand. "Get me outta here! Take me home with ya!"

But of course, to Maddie's ears, it was just the excited squeaking of a spunky little rodent. She giggled, charmed by his antics. "You're just the spunkiest little thing. I wish I could take you home with me, but I just can't."

With a final smile and a wave, she straightened up and walked away. "Take care, li'l guy!"

Clay scrambled at the glass, mirroring her position. "No! Come back, Maddie! Come back!" But it was no use. She was gone. Clay slumped against the glass, his tiny shoulders shaking with despair.

He was so lost in his misery that he didn't even notice the hand descending into the cage until it was too late. Suddenly, he was being lifted into the air, coming face to face with a grinning Bruce.

"Oh, aren't you just a little firecracker!" Bruce baby-talked, holding Clay up to his face. "Wish I could rescue all your brothers and sisters, but you'll have to do for now."

Clay squirmed in his grip, a sinking feeling in his gut. "Put me down, weirdo! Hey, wait a sec ... I know you from somewhere, don't I?"

A memory flashed through his mind — the bar, the awkward discussion, the dawning realization. Clay's eyes widened in horror. "Oh, no. Not him. Anyone but him!"

But it was too late. Bruce was already carrying him to the register, chatting excitedly with the clerk as he picked out an assortment of gerbil toys and accessories.

As he was unceremoniously dumped into a small cardboard carrier, Clay caught snatches of their conversation.

"...going to love his new home...got the deluxe habitrail all set up at home..."

Clay shuddered, panic rising in his throat. He had to get out of here. Though the accessories Bruce was purchasing for him looked like they could have been a lot of fun, he had way more important things to do; had to find that letter.

Thinking fast, he started chewing at the box, desperately trying to create an escape hatch. "This stuff tastes awful," he grumbled through a mouthful of cardboard. "But I'd chew my own dang leg off if I thought it'd get me outta here."

Just then, the lid of the box opened, and Clay found himself being unceremoniously dumped into some kind of globe.

"You're going to love this!" Bruce enthused, snapping the lid shut.

Clay blinked, taking in his new prison. It was a hamster ball, he realized — a transparent plastic sphere, just big enough for him to run around in.

For a moment, he just sat there, stunned. But then Bruce set the ball on the ground ... and Clay saw his chance.

"Alright, Brucie," he muttered. "You asked for it."

With a mighty kick of his hind legs, Clay sprinted, propelling the ball across the store floor, ricocheting off shelves and displays like a pinball on meth.

"Yeeehaw!" he crowed as startled customers leapt out of his way. "Now this is more like it!"

Distantly, he could hear Bruce and the clerk shouting, trying to corral him. But Clay was a gerbil possessed, zigging and zagging with wild abandon.

He nearly took out an old lady's ankle, sent a toddler sprawling into a stack of kibble, and upended a display of doggie sweaters. It was glorious chaos, and for a brief, shining moment, Clay felt a surge of hope.

Maybe, just maybe, he could pull this off. Maybe he could escape this hellish prison, find his way back to Maddie and the life he'd lost so long ago.

But then, disaster struck.

Just as Clay was making his triumphant dash for the automatic doors, a little boy appeared out of nowhere, his eyes wide with delight.

"Ball!" the kid screeched, chubby hands reaching out to snatch Clay's plastic chariot out of thin air.

Clay had just enough time to mutter a fervent prayer before the kid drop-kicked him like a little plastic soccer ball, sending him sailing out the door and into oncoming traffic.

In a heartbeat, Clay's world exploded into screeching tires and blaring horns, angry shouts and the stench of burning rubber.

He ricocheted off a bumper, went pinwheeling across the pavement, and nearly got flattened by a city bus. Sheer dumb luck and a few well-timed swerves were all that saved him from becoming roadkill.

By the time he bounced up onto the opposite curb, dangling at the edge of a concrete stairway, Clay felt like he'd aged a decade. His tiny body ached, his head was spinning, and he was pretty sure he'd pulled something in his little gerbil groin.

Then, before he could so much as catch his breath, Clay's sphere reached a tipping point and went tumbling downward, ass over teakettle.

The world spun in a sickening kaleidoscope of sky and stone, the plastic shell around him cracking a little more with every step's impact.

96

By the time he hit the bottom, Clay was seeing stars, and not the good kind.

The ball hit the pavement and exploded in a shower of plastic shards, sending Clay pinwheeling through the air like a furry little rocket. He bounced once, twice, and came to a bone-rattling stop against the leg of a park bench.

For a long moment, Clay just lay there, trying to remember how to breathe. Everything hurt — his head, his ribs, his bruised and battered dignity.

"Sweet Mercy," he managed to wheeze, spitting out a bloody tooth.

He struggled to his feet, fighting off a wave of nausea as the world tilted around him. He was just about to attempt a heroic, if slightly bow-legged, limp to safety when a shadow fell across him.

Slowly, dreading what he might see, Clay raised his eyes ... and found himself staring into the slitted pupils of a very hungry-looking tomcat.

"Oh, you gotta be kidding me," he groaned.

The cat crouched, its tail twitching, ready to pounce. Clay did the only thing he could think of; he turned tail and ran, scrambling up the leg of the bench like his fuzzy little butt was on fire.

The cat was hot on his heels, yowling and slashing with outstretched claws. But Clay was fueled by sheer, pants-wetting terror, and he managed to stay just a whisker ahead. The cat chased Clay, zigging, zagging, pouncing, swatting, all along the riverway path.

Clay shimmied up to the seat of another bench, then made a flying leap for the backrest. For one horrible moment, he hung suspended in midair, certain he'd misjudged the distance.

But then his paws hit wood, and he was scrambling up and over, his little heart going like a snare drum in his chest.

Behind him, he heard a yowl and a splash, and he glanced back just in time to see the cat, who had just leaped for him, hit the surface of the river below like a sack of wet cement.

A hysterical laugh bubbled up in Clay's throat. He'd done it. He'd actually done it. He'd looked death in the eye and lived to squeak the tale!

He did a little victory shimmy, shaking his fuzzy booty in the direction of his waterlogged would-be assassin.

"Ha! Take that, ya mangy feline! Teaches you to mess with a ... AAAAGH!!!"

A shadow blotted out the sun, a piercing shriek split the air and, suddenly, Clay was airborne — dangling from the razor-sharp talons of a very large, very determined hawk.

"Sweet mercy!" he yelped, his little legs churning uselessly beneath him.

The hawk carried him, higher and higher, and Clay could do nothing about it as he watched the city turn into the countryside below.

"Gabe, if this is another one of your little lessons, I swear to everything holy, I'll ... AAAAAAAIIIIEEEEEE!!!"

Just as Clay was certain he was soon to become a hairy hors d'oeuvre, a second hawk, plummeted out of nowhere, slamming into his captor like a guided missile.

Feathers flew. Beaks slashed and tore. Clay found himself caught between a pair of angry, squawking forces of nature, each determined to turn him into a midair snack, he reckoned.

But just as he was about to resign himself to becoming a very tenderized mouse burger, something unexpected happened. His original predator's talons slipped, letting loose and now he was gently in the grip of...Hawk Gabriel. He'd been saved!

Unfortunately, though, the other bird of prey wasn't a quitter and came screeching back, slamming into Gabriel.

... and suddenly, Clay was falling, plummeting towards what he was certain would be his final, inglorious end as a very small smear on the unforgiving earth below.

"AAAAAAUGH! GABRIEL!"

In his final moments, a sparkling glimmer caught his eye — a stream, snaking through the underbrush not far from where he was descending.

"Water!" he cried out in desperate relief. "Soft, wet, wonderful water! Please, Lord, just let me hit the water...!" The fact that Clay had never taken a physics course in his life was now evident.

Willing to try anything at this point, Clay positions himself aerodynamically, like a skydiver, and began blazing at a sharp angle, aiming towards the stream below.

Closer and closer the stream rushed up to meet him. This was it. He was going to make it. He was actually going to ...

... just then Clay noticed the biggest dang buck he'd ever seen sauntering up to the stream to take a glorious sip. Its backside directly in line with Clay's trajectory.

Hearing the sonic whistle of Clay rifling towards him, the buck raised its head, then its ears, then its ... tail.

Clay's tiny body was hurtling at terminal velocity towards the puckered bullseye of the deer's unsuspecting sphincter. He tried to correct his course, but the kinetic force was in control now.

In that instant, his life flashed before his eyes. His childhood. His parents. Maddie. All the choices, all the mistakes that had brought him to this final, juicy end, this literal cosmic buttstravaganza.

He almost welcomed it, in a way. Embraced the sweet release of oblivion, the absolution found in complete and utter defeat.

But once again, fate had other plans.

Just as Clay was about to be launched where no gerbil had gone before, a flash of movement caught his eye. A swooping, feathered form, cutting through the air like an avenging angel.

It was Hawk Gabriel again. He'd come to snatch Clay from the jaws of inglorious rectal doom.

In a heartbeat, Clay felt those familiar talons close around his battered body, felt himself being yanked up and away, his fuzzy cheeks flapping in the wind.

"Thanks ... I think." he squeaked, peering up at Gabriel through shell-shocked eyes.

The hawk just winked, somehow managing a shrug with his wings.

"You're welcome," he replied. "Though I gotta say ... that was a real slobberknocker of an entrance you almost made there."

Clay shuddered, his butthole clenching in phantom sympathy. "Well, if anyone asks, that never happened. Let's not get all gossipy, ok?"

"No promises," Gabriel chuckled darkly. But there was a fondness in his predatory gaze, an almost fatherly pride as he carried Clay up and away, back towards the one place he'd never thought he'd be so glad to see.

Home.

Pastor Matt was standing on the sidewalk, frozen in his tracks and watching as the hawk gently deposited its tiny cargo in Clay's front yard. The entire scene had an almost surreal quality — a predator bird playing nursemaid to a gerbil? He raised the back of his hand to his forehead, checking for fever.

"Clay," Matt muttered, shaking his head, "what did you put in that moonshine of yours?"

Meanwhile, Gerbil Clay scampered up the front steps of his ruined home, squeezing through a crack in the door without a backward glance. Inside, he hugged the baseboard, his tiny heart still racing from his aerial adventure. As he rounded a corner, he came face-to-face with a mouse.

"Well, hello there, li'l feller," Clay greeted, somewhat amused by the role reversal. Here he was, usually the hunter, now barely bigger than his typical prey.

The mouse squeaked at him, gesturing with its nose for Clay to follow. Something in its manner seemed almost ... purposeful. Intrigued, Clay followed as his newfound guide led him across the room.

They reached the far wall, where the mouse pointed proudly to a mousetrap, loaded with an enormous — from their perspective — hunk of cheese. The mouse inched forward, whiskers twitching as it sniffed at the tempting bait.

A jolt of recognition shot through Clay. He knew exactly what was about to happen.

"No! Wait!" he cried out, but it was too late.

SNAP!

The trap sprung with lethal efficiency, but through some miracle, the cheese went flying, landing intact right in front of Clay. He stared at it for a long moment, his tiny conscience wrestling with his rumbling stomach.

"Ohhhh," he sighed, then picked up the cheese, taking a tentative nibble. "Well, I guess one mouse's misfortune is another mouse's dinner," he rationalized around a mouthful of cheddar. "Boy, am I starvin'!"

After wolfing down the last few bites, Clay made his way back across the room to his old bedroom door. He squeezed underneath, his heart leaping when he spotted what he'd been hoping to find.

There, lying innocently on the floor next to the wall, was Maddie's letter.

"Thank you, Lord!" Clay exclaimed, doing a little victory dance. "I got it. I finally got it!"

In his excitement, he grabbed the letter in his teeth, trying to carry it in front of him. But the envelope was comically large from his rodent perspective, causing him to stumble and trip. Undeterred, Clay circled around to the other side, took it in his mouth again, and began dragging it backward like a determined puppy with an oversized stick.

He was so focused on his prize, so caught up in his moment of triumph, that he didn't notice where his backward journey was taking him. Didn't see the second mousetrap until it was too late.

SNAP!

In a flash of cosmic irony, Clay found himself back in Heaven, materializing in a puff of smoke not too far from his ever-dwindling candle. His body was frozen in place, eyes bulging cartoonishly, but at least he was in human form again. Gabriel stood nearby, clearly struggling to maintain his celestial composure.

"Welcome back, Ordell," the angel managed, his lips twitching suspiciously.

Clay gradually regained his ability to move, eyeing Gabriel with suspicion. "Did I miss something funny?"

"I apologize," Gabriel said, though his eyes still danced with barely suppressed mirth. "But you were the one who set all those traps."

"I had it!" Clay exploded, looking down at his now-empty hands in despair. "I had the letter! It was in my grasp!"

He trudged over to stand beside Gabriel in front of the candle, his shoulders slumped in defeat.

"So," Gabriel asked, his voice gentle but probing, "did you learn anything?"

Clay's temper flared. "Oh yeah, well I learned that having your neck snapped in a mousetrap is a whole lot more painful than your fingers when you're trying to set the damn thing!" He glared at the angel accusingly. "What kind of ... I mean, I had the letter. Why couldn't you just let me have that?"

Gabriel raised an eyebrow. "I'm sorry, maybe I missed something. Is that letter magical or something? A talisman?"

"You told me," Clay insisted, confusion creeping into his voice. "You told me that the letter holds the key to what I'm lacking."

"Well, in a manner of speaking, I guess you could say that," Gabriel conceded. "But if I recall, I said something like, 'find the *spirit* of what's in her letter and you will be restored.'"

Clay threw up his hands in frustration. "Well alright then, that's what I'm fixin' to do if y'all would just stop kickin' my butt for a moment."

Then another thought struck him, "Oh, and what's up with that Bruce guy?"

"What do you mean?"

"You know," Clay said, making a dismissive gesture, "all that tree-huggin', animal-lovin' nonsense. He's one of them PETA people, ain't he?"

When Gabriel remained silent; Clay elaborated, "Bruce? All that 'bacon is murder' stuff?"

Gabriel's expression hardened slightly. "Bruce is one of God's children. Are you more special, more compassionate than he?" Clay felt shame; he didn't have a good response.

The angel turned his attention back to the candle, and Clay followed his gaze. The flame guttered slightly; the wax noticeably shorter than before. The sight sobered him.

"OK, so I get it," Clay said quickly. "Everyone deserves a fair shot. Everyone is important. I've learned my lesson, so can I just get on with my harp strummin' now?" He gestured hopefully toward the pearly gates.

When Gabriel didn't respond, Clay grew more insistent. "Sweet mercy, I'm fixed already. Ya fixed me."

"Oh?" Gabriel's voice dripped skepticism.

104

"Yeah, I understand now. I should probably be more thoughtful. More sensitive to people and critters."

Gabriel looked solemnly at the candle, clasping his hands behind his back. Clay's heart sank as he realized this test wasn't over.

"Well, you did try to stop that mouse from getting crushed by your trap," Gabriel acknowledged, "but that's not quite the whole picture."

"Why not?" Clay protested. "I tried to do a good deed."

"It's not necessarily about just doing good deeds."

"No? What's all that stuff in the bible about do this and don't do that then? I gotta change my ways and be good, or you'll roast me."

Gabriel shook his head. "That's not what it says. The question is, *why* did you try to do a good deed?"

"Cuz I'm tired of the beatdown!" Clay exploded. "I wanna get in there and see my folks. You guys are just too hard to please. What do I have to do to get in? Tell me, please!"

Gabriel's voice was gentle but firm. "There's nothing you could ever do, Clay, to earn God's favor."

The words hit Clay like a physical blow. He deflated, his anger dissolving into confusion and despair.

"Well then I guess I'm screwed," he said quietly. "What's the point of all this then? Why send me back if there's nothin' I can do about it?"

Gabriel remained silent; his eyes fixed on the guttering candle. Clay rallied for one last attempt.

"Maybe if you'd send me back as somethin' normal, I might be able to figure this thing out," he suggested hopefully.

Gabriel made a gesture with his hand as if telling Clay to keep going.

Clay obliged. "Well, ya keep sending me back as a wild animal, out there in nature where everything's tryin' to kill me or eat me?"

"I'm listening"

"Maybe send me back as a zoo animal or something; they at least get taken care of. Or how about something that has more abilities." Clay's eyes lit up with desperate inspiration, wiggling his hands in front of him. "Like maybe something with opposable thumbs so I can open a letter for Pete's sake."

A disquieting gleam entered Gabriel's eyes that made Clay immediately regret his words. His stomach dropped as he recognized that all-too-familiar look.

"Deal!" Gabriel declared with unsettling enthusiasm.

Clay began backing away, waving his arms in front of him. "On second thought ...."

But it was too late. The wheels were already in motion, and Clay was about to discover that sometimes, you should be very careful what you wish for.

10 - The Primate's Progress

Clay materialized once again on the planet, the sun just starting to peek over the horizon. Warm water enveloped him as gentle hands worked shampoo through his fur. Through the steam rising from the bath, Clay caught sight of his reflection in a nearby mirror and did a double-take as realization dawned. There he was, covered in dark fur, his face transformed into that of a chimpanzee.

"Well I'll be a monkey's uncle," Clay marveled internally. Then he saw who his attendant was, "Maddie? Maddie! Sweet mercy, you sure get around!"

Unlike his previous transformations, which had felt like cosmic jokes at his expense, this one offered an unexpected gift — the chance to be close to her again, even if she didn't know who he really was.

Her touch was professional but kind, each movement precise and purposeful, yet filled with a tenderness that made his throat tight. This was pure Maddie — the girl who'd always seen the best in everyone and everything, now grown into a woman who'd made caring for others her life's work.

Clay studied her face. She hummed softly as she worked, some tune he didn't recognize, but the peaceful expression she wore was achingly familiar. It was the same look she'd had all those years ago when they'd play veterinarian in his backyard, tending to neighborhood pets with Band-Aids and baby aspirin.

"You're going to feel so much better once we get you cleaned up," she murmured, scratching behind his ears in a way that made his eyes roll back in pleasure. "There we go, sweet boy. See? Nothing to be afraid of."

The irony wasn't lost on Clay — here he was, closer to Maddie than he'd been in twenty years, and he couldn't tell her a thing. But maybe that was the point. Maybe he needed to just listen. Maybe he needed to remember how to be truly seen before he could learn how to be truly known again.

Across the room, Bobby, a freshman in the research program, cast furtive glances their way, his clipboard forgotten in his hands. Clay recognized the look in the young researcher's eyes — who wouldn't fall a little bit in love with Maddie? She had that effect on people. Always had.

"Aaaaah," he thought to himself. "I finally died and gone to heaven."

As Maddie continued to bathe him, Clay became increasingly aware of his state of undress. "Ho! Wait a sec, I'm naked, Maddie. We ain't even had a first date yet."

Across the room, Bobby was still sneaking glances their way, his eyes holding a mix of scientific fascination and unmistakable jealousy as he watched Maddie's tender ministrations.

Maddie reached for a towel, preparing to lift Clay from the tub. "Let's get you all dried off, shall we?" Clay snatched the towel, trying to

108

maintain some level of modesty, and hastily covered his 'giblets' as he liked to call them.

"You silly! Shy, are we?" She giggled and reclaimed control of the towel. As she gloriously wiped him down, Clay found himself distracted, playing with Maddie's curls.

Just then, David, the department head, entered the lab. "Hey, Madelyn. How's it coming? Getting him all cleaned up?" he asked.

Maddie beamed with excitement. "I sure am, Boss. I'm so excited! This is a giant step up from rats."

"Yes, it sure is...isn't it, Bobby?" David replied, with an air of superiority, glancing over at the rookie.

Bobby, who had been feeding a small food pellet to a rat in a cage, looked up resentfully, yet in check, towards his authority.

Maddie continued to towel off Clay, and David turned his attention to the chimpanzee.

"OK, here are your objectives, all laid out for you," David said, placing a folder on the table beside Maddie. "Take as much time as you need. Did you already give him his testosterone booster shots?"

Maddie secured a diaper around Clay's waist. "Yep, all set."

"Perfect," David said, heading for the door.

Maddie lifted Clay, holding him up in front of her. He reached out, wanting to be closer to her. She pulled him in for a hug.

"Boy, you sure are friendly today," Maddie laughed.

As the day progressed, Maddie presented Clay with a series of cognitive tests and puzzles. With each successful completion, Clay reveled in Maddie's praise and attention.

"Gooood boooy! Wow! That's my good boy!"

"Pastor Matt was right," Clay thought to himself smugly. "I ain't so dim after all."

Clay's eagerness to impress Maddie knew no bounds. After solving a particularly challenging puzzle, he leaped into her arms, pushing aside the proffered banana reward in favor of a more personal token of affection. Maddie giggled, playfully fending off his amorous advances.

As the sun began to set, Maddie secured Clay in his enclosure for the night. She bid him goodnight, flipping off the lights as she and Bobby prepared to leave.

Clay grabbed the bars of his cage, rattling them in frustration. "Oh, it's OK, Casanova. I'll see you again in the morning," Maddie called over her shoulder.

Clay watched her leave, his heart aching with the need to express himself. "Help me, Maddie! I need another chance," he silently pleaded. "I need your help! I'm being held captive by an angel with a dangerous sense of humor!"

But his cries went unheard, his words trapped behind the barrier of his animal form. As the lab grew quiet, Clay resigned himself to another night alone with his thoughts.

"Dadjimmit!"

Clay turned to survey his cage, and his eyes fell upon his cellmate — a female chimpanzee eyeing him with unmistakable interest.

"Sweet Mercy! Don't even think about it, you hussy!"

The next morning, Maddie arrived at the lab and, with inexplicable astonishment, found the chimp sitting at Bobby's desk with a bag of chips in one hand and a beer in the other. On the TV screen, a rerun of *Baywatch* played, the sound muted.

"Buddy!" Maddie exclaimed; her shock evident.

Clay froze, his eyes darting to the clock on the wall. 5:30 AM. He hadn't expected Maddie for at least another hour.

"Maddie, you're early," he thought, chagrined at being caught red-handed.

Maddie's gaze traveled from Clay to the TV, then to the female chimpanzee watching forlornly from the locked enclosure. Her mouth fell open as she struggled to process the scene before her.

Clay braced himself for a scolding, but instead, Maddie rushed over and scooped him into her arms. As she held him close, he noticed her eyes were red and puffy, as if she'd been sad.

"You been cryin'? What's wrong?" He reached up, gently wiping away a stray tear.

Maddie carried him over to a plush armchair in the corner, sinking down into it with Clay cradled in her lap. She sniffled, her voice thick with emotion as she spoke.

"Oh, you're so sweet. I need a friend like you right now. I wish I could talk to you. I wish you could understand."

Clay listened intently, his heart aching for her. "Well, why not?" Maddie continued, "I can share it with you. You're a good listener."

As Maddie poured out her heart, Clay felt a wave of empathy wash over him. He learned that she was grieving a friend who had lost his way, someone who had once been happy and full of life but had succumbed to his inner demons.

"Why didn't he reach out for help? Why did he try to bear his own burdens?" Maddie lamented.

Clay listened, his mind racing. "Oh, Maddie. I gotta figure this thing out. I know Gabriel said there wasn't anything magical about your letter, but it's the only thing I can think of to get a clue."

He gazed into Maddie's eyes, trying to convey his understanding.

"I gotta break free from this. I gotta break free." The phrase resounded, over and over, in Clay's mind like an earworm.

The infamous 'Queen' lyrics played in his head, continuously, during the following days filled with a blur of tests, triumphs, and increasingly bold escape attempts.

Maddie stood before a flip chart covered with various colored circles, squares, and triangles, her face lighting up as Clay correctly identified each shape she named. His reward was her radiant smile and the careful notes she made on her clipboard.

Later, seated in Maddie's lap, Clay watched her place a ball under one of three cups. His eyes tracked her hands as she shuffled them, and without hesitation, he picked the right one. His reward wasn't the offered banana—instead, he planted a quick kiss on her cheek, earning a delighted laugh. He repeated this performance several times, each success bringing them closer together.

Another morning found Maddie entering the lab to discover Clay had once again escaped his enclosure. This time she found him rummaging through the refrigerator, a *NASCAR* race playing on the TV in the background. His subsequent confinement in a now-padlocked pen left him sulking, staring dejectedly at a banana while his female cage-mate picked through his fur.

During one test, Maddie held up four fingers and mouthed the word "four." Instead of selecting the corresponding number of apples from the basket before him, Clay spotted the bouquet on her desk. He plucked exactly four flowers and presented them to her with a winning smile.

Clay watched as David reviewed Maddie's results, the head researcher's arm slipping around her shoulders in a congratulatory gesture that seemed to linger way too long. Bobby looked on with barely concealed jealousy, while Clay expressed his own displeasure by sending a carefully constructed Jenga tower clattering across the table. David was lucky Clay didn't have to poop at the moment, he thought.

The nights brought their own adventures. The bored security guard became a regular visitor, unlocking Clay's pen for marathon poker sessions fueled by beer and whatever sporting event was playing on pay TV. Clay grew to anticipate these visits, though the guard's increasing comfort with their arrangement would later prove useful.

Maddie's creativity in testing Clay's abilities seemed boundless. One day found him gleefully attacking a Whack-A-Mole game, while another day she attempted to motivate him with a banana dangling from the ceiling tiles. Clay's response was to pass the banana by and instead raid Bobby's lunch from the refrigerator, settling down to enjoy his stolen meal with exaggerated satisfaction.

The security guard's late-night visits continued to escalate. Empty beer cans accumulated around them as they played cards, Clay's artificially loud belch earning a hearty laugh from his increasingly intoxicated companion.

During one particularly memorable afternoon, David burst into the lab, making a beeline for Bobby's desk. He slammed down a cable bill, jabbing his finger at a long list of Pay-Per-View charges — *WWE Wrestlemania*, *UFC* events, and more. As Bobby stammered denials, David's threat of "One more chance" hung in the air. Clay tried to direct Maddie's attention back to their puzzle, adopting his most innocent expression when she looked at him suspiciously.

When Maddie presented him with a mixed-up Rubik's cube, Clay took one look at it, shook his head, and handed it back. Even he knew better than to attempt that particular challenge.

His nights with the security guard had evolved into a carefully orchestrated routine. Clay would pull out a poker chip case while his companion hauled in a cooler of beer. With practiced hospitality, Clay would fetch cold ones for the guard but deliberately abstain himself, his mind focused on the longer game.

Though he intentionally lost hand after hand, Clay made sure to keep the guard's spirits high and his glass full. The man celebrated each victory with increasingly enthusiastic swigs, Clay faithfully replacing empty bottles with fresh ones. As the hours wore on, the guard's decision-making grew steadily worse, his celebrations more boisterous.

After a particularly long session, Clay dealt what he knew would be the final hand. The guard's bleary eyes lit up at the sight of his pocket aces, and he pushed all his chips to the center of the table with drunken confidence. Clay made a show of considering his cards before calling the bet. The flop brought two queens and an eight, followed by a five, and finally — the last queen on the river.

The guard let out a triumphant laugh, slapping his aces onto the table. But his victory was short-lived; his head slowly dropped to the table with a soft thud, finally succumbing to Clay's patient strategy.

Clay pushed back from the table and approached the unconscious guard, carefully lifting and dropping his hand to confirm he was truly out. Satisfied, he took the guard's jacket and gently placed it under his head as a pillow. He retrieved the keys from the man's belt with the delicate touch of a professional pickpocket.

As he turned to leave, Clay paused, remembering one last detail. He returned to the table and flipped over his own cards, revealing the fourth queen. With a satisfied smirk, he pulled all the chips to his side before making his exit.

The cool night air hit Clay as he emerged from the University Lab building. His eyes fell on a moped parked nearby, and within moments he had it hot-wired. The engine sputtered to life, and Clay felt the first true taste of freedom since his transformation as he sped away.

Dawn was just breaking as Pastor Matt emerged from his house, glancing furtively in both directions before proceeding with exaggerated stealth toward Clay's property. From his bathrobe pocket, he produced a brand-new Holy Water Sprinkler and its accompanying instruction pamphlet. Being a Baptist preacher, Pastor Matt had no idea what he was doing; he just knew something wasn't right next-door and certainly a cleansing couldn't hurt. After a quick consultation with the manual, he began solemnly sprinkling the charred house, moving methodically every few feet.

The relative silence of early morning was broken by the sputtering approach of a moped. Matt caught the movement in his peripheral vision and turned just in time to see a chimpanzee riding down the sidewalk. He did a double-take, flinching as if physically struck by the absurdity of the sight.

Clay simply waved as he dismounted the moped, calling out, "Mornin' Pastor," though of course it emerged as nothing more than a cheerful primate grunt. He headed purposefully toward the backyard while Pastor Matt stood frozen, holy water sprinkler suspended in mid-air.

After a moment, Matt wordlessly tossed the sprinkler and pamphlet over his shoulder and retreated back to own his house.

Inside Clay's house, the chimp made a beeline to where he last held the letter. To his surprise, though, the letter was missing and only a slab of gerbil jerky remained. He had a meltdown, waving his arms frantically, bouncing off the walls and screaming in chimpese, "It's that dadjim armadilla again. I'd bet my last banana!"

Inside Maddie's apartment across town, a phone was ringing. She startled awake, fumbling for the receiver.

"Hello? Yes?" Her eyes flew open as she absorbed the news. "What? He escaped? But how?" She bolted upright in bed. "Yes, I'll be right there."

Meanwhile, Clay had reached the armadillo's tree den in his backyard. He crouched down at the base of what remained of the old oak — now just a blackened stump — and peered into the hole.

"Here's Clay!" he thought, channeling his best Jack Nicholson as he poked his head down into the darkness.

Inside his house, Pastor Matt was attempting to process the morning's events over a cup of coffee. He reluctantly turned to look out his window into Clay's backyard. Without changing his expression, he turned his back from the window and leaned against the counter. The sound of three beeps broke the silence as he raised his cell phone to his ear.

After a moment, a tinny voice responded: "911, what is the emergency?"

"Yes, there's a monkey riding an armadillo next door," Matt reported with eerily calm detachment.

Through the window behind him, the scene played out exactly as described — a chimpanzee was indeed attempting to ride the armadillo like a bucking bronco across the yard. The armadillo had Maddie's letter clenched firmly in its mouth.

Outside the chaos continued.

"Give it up! Give it up!" Clay's frustrated thoughts emerged as determined grunts as he switched to professional wrestler mode. He planted his feet firmly and brought the armadillo's escape attempt to an abrupt halt. With a surge of strength, he hoisted the creature above his head and executed a perfect dropping back breaker move. The armadillo bounced off Clay's knee and fell to the ground, dazed but still maintaining its grip on the precious letter.

Clay tried to delicately remove the letter from the armadillo's unyielding grip. "Now, dang it, let go," he silently pleaded. "Don't be tearin' it up. Just let go." But the armadillo's jaw remained firmly clamped on its prize, and Clay, not wanting to risk damaging the letter further, was forced to reconsider his strategy.

"Alright, you asked for it."

After a quick survey of his surroundings, Clay clambered up the side of his house to the windowsill. With the calculated precision of a wrestling superstar, he launched himself into an elbow hammer move aimed directly at his opponent. At the last moment, however, the crafty creature rolled itself into a tight ball, causing Clay to miss his target and crash painfully to the ground.

Through his window, Pastor Matt continued his surreal conversation with emergency services, maintaining his unnaturally calm demeanor as he watched the spectacle unfold. His wife stood behind him, her eyes bulging in amazement as Clay now utilized the armadillo like a soccer ball, displaying remarkable athleticism as he bounced it off his knees, then his head, before executing a perfect back-flip Pele kick that sent the armored creature crashing into the fence.

The impact finally dislodged the letter from the armadillo's mouth. Dazed and defeated, the creature shook its head groggily before wobbling back toward its den.

"Yes! Yes!" Clay's victory celebration came out as a series of excited hoots. "Ha ha! Oh, Maddie, we did it!"

After catching his breath, Clay reached for the letter with trembling hands. As he began to slide his finger into the corner of the envelope, the screech of tires brought his head up sharply. Through the fence, he spotted a police cruiser, and two officers were already making their way toward the yard.

"Really?" Clay looked skyward in exasperation. "Really?"

With a resigned sigh, he tucked the letter into his mouth and sprang to his feet. The officers closed in, but Clay's agility served him well as he juked and weaved before deciding to make a leap over the back fence. The officers gave chase, pursuing him across the street and into a park.

In her car, Maddie was breaking the speed limit, listening to a morning radio show when the personality broke in with a news bulletin.

"We just received word that there's a chimpanzee on the loose in the city. If you're on the northeast side of town, keep your eyes peeled as police are trying to capture the animal."

"Oh, Buddy," Maddie whispered, her voice tight with concern. Seconds later, she slammed on her brakes as Clay himself darted across the street in front of her car, the pursuing officers close behind. "Buddy!"

Clay rounded the corner of a city block, quickly scanning his surroundings before his gaze locked onto a tall city square statue under construction. Without hesitation, he made for it. Moments later, the panting officers rounded the same corner and continued their pursuit.

Reaching the base of the statue, Clay glanced back at the closing officers before beginning his climb. Meanwhile, Maddie's car screeched around the corner. She pulled over and jumped out, joining the growing crowd of onlookers.

Clay reached the top of the statue and leaned against the figurine, catching his breath. Below, the crowd continued to grow, including Maddie who called out desperately.

"Buddy! What are you doing? You come down here right now!"

"Sorry, Maddie," Clay thought, his chest still heaving. "I gotta do this. It's a matter of life or death."

As Clay began to unfold the letter, something wet struck the statue beside him. He looked up to find the source of the pigeon dropping and locked eyes with a familiar presence perched atop the statue's head.

"So, you finally have the letter," Pigeon Gabriel observed.

"Yeah, no thanks to you," Clay retorted internally. "Why did it have to be so difficult?"

"Why is the letter so important to you?"

"It's Maddie's. It's from Maddie. You said yourself it'll restore everything."

"Never said that, but what is it about Maddie that's so special?"

Clay felt his frustration mounting. "You ask some really dumb questions, you know that? One moment you tell me one thing, like how Maddie is one of your favorites, but then in the next breath you ask me why I think she's so special. You don't make no sense half the time."

"Oh, she is very special, no doubt of that," Gabriel conceded. "But why do *you* think she's so special?"

Clay's expression softened as he considered the question. "She's special. I don't know, I mean she's kind; she loves everything and everyone. She's always so happy. She never lets anything get to her. She's so easy-going, no matter what happens around her. She can be sad about somethin', but still has a smile goin' on inside."

"So, then why do you need that letter so badly?" Gabriel pressed. "You know that Maddie is special. You don't need a letter to prove that to you, do you? You know her. She's always been so much more than a silly piece of paper."

Clay looked down at the letter in his hands, doubt creeping into his expression.

"Now climb down from here before momma and papa swallow return," Gabriel warned. "They don't like anyone messing with their babies."

Clay noticed a small nest with baby swallows resting in the bent elbow of the statue. Pigeon Gabriel took flight, leaving Clay alone with his thoughts.

"Oh Maddie, why did you ever have to leave?" Clay stared at the letter, his heart aching. "I ain't been the same since you gone. I wanna be the same that I was before. Like when I was with you."

A sharp impact to his head interrupted his reflection. "Ouch! What the—?"

Looking up, Clay found himself face to face with two very angry swallows, who began taking turns diving at his head. In his effort to fend them off, the letter slipped from his grasp.

From above, the scene resembled something out of an old monster movie—Clay swatting at the diving birds from his tower as they executed precision attacks, the crowd below watching in horrified fascination. All that was missing were the biplanes.

Driven to his knees by the relentless assault, Clay spotted the letter inching dangerously close to the ledge. He reached for it desperately, but at that exact moment, one of the swallows delivered a particularly well-aimed poke to his rear end. Clay's reflexive jerk was all it took — the letter caught a breeze and fluttered away from the statue.

"Nooo!"

The crowd below gasped collectively as Clay lunged for the letter, overbalancing in the process. Time seemed to slow as he toppled from his perch, the ground rushing up to meet him with terrible finality. He hit with a sickening thud, the impact driving the air from his lungs.

Through blurring vision, Clay saw Maddie rushing to his side, tears already streaming down her face. He tried to focus on her beauty one last time before darkness began creeping in at the edges of his consciousness.

A voice from the crowd broke through his fading awareness: ""Twas Beauty killed the beast."

The bystander glanced around hopefully, waiting for someone to appreciate his cinematic reference, but was met with only uncomfortable silence.

As Clay's world faded to black, his last coherent thought was of Maddie's smile—not the tears he saw now, but the bright, hopeful grin of their shared childhood. The one that had made him feel like anything was possible.

At least he'd tried. At least he'd ....

The world dissolved around him, replaced by the familiar ethereal glow of Heaven. He found himself staring at Gabriel, who stood beside the small stub of a candle. Clay's physical form flickered as it solidified, like a TV with poor reception finally finding its signal.

With painful effort and a helping hand from Gabriel, Clay rose to his feet.

Clay thought back to his moments with Maddie, the way she'd cared for him, trusted him, even if she hadn't known who he really was.

Gabriel engaged Clay, bringing him back to the task at hand, "How was life as a chimp, Clay? Learn anything?"

"Being a chimp ain't all bad, I guess" he admitted grudgingly. "Once you get past the whole 'being locked in a cage with a horny chimpette thing."

Gabriel laughed, a smile playing at the corners of his mouth, continuing with the levity. "And you gotta admit, riding that armadillo like a bucking bronco had to be fun. And the smackdown? That's right up your alley. Am I right?"

Clay couldn't help but briefly re-live the whoop he finally got to put on that dadjim critter. He chuckled.

Clay was ushered back to the seriousness of his situation; anxious about the dwindling candle. By the looks of things, he may only have one more shot at this thing.

Clay felt a surge of desperation, his mind casting about for some lifeline, some trump card to play. "Look, I found the letter. I completed my mission. I kept my end of the bargain; can't I just go in there and rest now?"

Gabriel sighed, "You put so much stock in that one little letter. Well, it's gone now Clay. The letter is disintegrating in some landfill now. It was never about the letter anyway; you're still missing the point."

Something in Clay snapped, the last of his bravado crumbling away. "OK, I give up! I'm going to let you in on a little secret, Gabriel. I'm not the sharpest bulb in the drawer. My 'telligence quote ain't exactly tip-top. So, I'm gonna need some help with all this! Help me, Gabriel!"

He paused, his voice dropping to a hoarse whisper. "Please."

The angel's eyes lit up, a smile spreading across his face. "Now we're getting somewhere! First off, Clay, don't be so hard on yourself. You're not as dim as you think. Much of what I'm trying to teach you, you already know. You just need to own those thoughts for yourself, recognize what's already planted inside of you."

He laid a hand on Clay's shoulder, the touch sending a jolt of warmth through his weary bones. "Life is a vapor, Clay. Humanity is like drops of dew on the grass, gone before morning reaches noon. No flesh lives forever. Sooner or later, the Creator brings back to Himself what He has given. Some live long lives, some are brought back to Him much sooner..."

"And some get blowed up with an armadilla?" Clay interjected, a wry twist to his mouth.

Gabriel laughed, a sound like summer rain. "Yeah, I suppose that could happen."

"I reckon I shortened earth's life-expectancy with that one," Clay surmised, "That was quite a bit of carbon I spewed there."

"Quite," Gabriel agreed.

"That's got me wonderin', since you know everything," Clay pondered, "what's up with this global warmin' stuff? Is that for real, or just a load of bullsh...crap?"

"Concern for the environment, Clay?" Gabriel questioned. "What does it matter to you? I could tell you the planet only has a few more years left before its tipping-point, or I could tell you it's all been politicized to redistribute wealth and gain power over others. Does the answer really matter to you?"

Clay scratched his head.

"Either way," the angel continued, "don't you think you should keep your room clean?"

Clay sobered; the point made sense. "So, what now?"

"There's still something you lack," Gabriel said, his gaze piercing. "You've shown some signs of progress, but you still haven't found what you've lost. Not fully. But you're close, Clay. So close."

"Maybe I'd get even closer if you'd help me out a bit," Clay suggested hopefully.

Gabriel's interest seemed to pique at this.

Encouraged, Clay pressed on. "Yeah! I mean, you send me back as a cockroach, a duck, a gerbil, a chimp? What the heck! Why don't ya give me a fightin' chance?"

"Such as?"

"Well, send me back as something bigger. Better." Clay's eyes lit up with desperate inspiration. "Send me back as something with cajónes; something with real teeth."

Then he saw it again. That mischievous look in the angel's eye as his celestial gears were churning in his head.

"I sure don't like that look in your eye...but...I'm ready," Clay said with resolve. "Go ahead. Kick my ass into the vortex again. I don't care anymore. I ain't got much time. Send me back as whatever you like."

He closed his eyes, bracing for the rush of celestial power that would propel him back to the land of the living. Back to his final chance at redemption.

But when the divine hurricane failed to materialize, Clay cracked one eye open, confused. Gabriel was watching him expectantly, a mischievous glint in his gaze.

"Well?" Clay asked, a tinge of impatience creeping into his voice. "What're you waiting for?"

"Oh, my hands-on approach, you know, tossing you violently back to earth ... that was just for my own amusement," Gabriel admitted with a wink. "Much more fun that way. But all I really need to do is .... "

He thrust his hand forward, doing his best Captain Picard impression. "Computer, lay in a course for Earth. Engage."

Clay stumbled back a step, the implication hitting him like a freight train — all this time, all the hurtling through space and unceremonious crash landings.

But before he could form a sufficiently indignant response, Gabriel's expression turned deadly serious as Clay's body began to stretch and blur. "No more last chances, Clay. No more excuses. It's time to make it happen."

The world began to fade around the edges, Heaven's ethereal glow giving way to the muted tones of earthly existence. As Clay felt himself being transported back into the mortal realm, peacefully and painlessly this time, Gabriel's parting words echoed in Clay's ears; a final challenge and benediction all in one, "Find what you've lost, Clay. Find it, and find yourself. Your future, your very soul ...."

11 - Hounded by the Past

Clay blinked, taking stock of his surroundings; the interior of a van, the low hum of an engine, the pungent scent of sweat and anticipation. Wearing a protective vest, complete with an official SWAT team badge, his German Shepherd body was seated among a group of men. Their faces were tense with concentration.

"Sweet Mercy," Clay muttered to himself, catching a glimpse of his reflection in the van's window. "I'm a cop!"

The SWAT leader, a grizzled man with a cigar clamped between his teeth, was outlining the impending operation, his voice a low, urgent rumble. Clay listened with half an ear, his mind still reeling from Gabriel's haunting, last message.

"The targets are suspected of running a massive drug operation in the old helium factory on the west side," the leader explained, jabbing a finger at a whiteboard. "They're using this site as a cover to push some nitrous, aka laughing gas, in balloons, to our teens."

Clay's ears perked up at that, a flicker of indignation sparking in his chest. Pushing drugs on kids? That was lower than a snake's belly in a wagon rut.

The leader droned on, outlining entry points and team positions. Clay found his attention drifting, his mind wandering back to the life he'd left behind. The weight of his failures pressed down on him, a physical ache in his chest.

Suddenly, the leader's voice caught Clay's attention, "Instead of our standard percussion grenades, our newest member here," he said, while grabbing and shaking Clay's harness, "will enter the window, breaching entry and creating the diversion."

Clay gulped, the implications sinking in. "What?" he yelped, forgetting for a moment that his words would fall on deaf ears. "You want *me* to go in first? I'm the front line?"

But the briefing continued, heedless of his protests. The van rumbled to a stop, and the team began to mobilize, checking weapons and adjusting gear. Clay felt a rising tide of panic, his heart hammering against his ribs.

This wasn't what he'd signed up for. He was a varmint control specialist, not some gung-ho SWAT dog. He'd barely survived his last few misadventures — the bird of prey, the armadillo cage match, his ill-fated flights as Clay the duck. And now they expected him to take point on a drug bust?

But as the team filed out of the van, falling into formation with practiced ease, Clay felt a flicker of something else beneath the fear. A sense of purpose, of rightness. He may not have chosen this path, but he was here for a reason. Maybe, just maybe, this was his chance to make a difference. To be the kind of man — or dog — that Maddie always believed he could be.

With a deep breath, Clay fell into step beside his handler, his senses sharpening as they approached the looming bulk of the factory. The

128

scent of danger hung heavy in the air, mingling with the acrid tang of chemicals and the sickly-sweet odor of nitrous oxide.

As the team took their positions, Clay could feel the weight of expectation settling on his shoulders. He thought of Maddie, of the person he was slowly becoming through all these transformations.

And in that moment, something shifted inside him. A tiny, imperceptible click, like a key turning in a lock. A door, creaking open.

Clay watched as Delta team members scaled the sides of the factory. From his position, he could see them cutting through the roof with silenced drills, inserting remote video equipment. A flash of mirror signals glinted between the teams.

"We've got eyes. Stand by," came Beta Leader's voice over the comms.

Alpha team huddled outside the factory's fence, SWAT Leader at point. He signaled 'eyes' to his men, and Clay could feel the tension ratcheting up another notch.

Inside the van, Beta team monitored their video feeds, confirming the targets processing balloons. Guards stood post throughout the factory.

"Bingo," Beta Leader's voice crackled over the radio. "We're clear. The southwest quadrant is secure. Get the K9 into position."

SWAT Leader signaled to Alpha 1, who had Clay on a leash, to move into position. But as his handler started down the fence row, Clay planted his feet, refusing to budge. Stage fright kicked in with a vengeance.

"Forget that. I ain't your dang guinea pig," Clay thought, his old stubbornness flaring. "Besides, I ain't got time for this."

Alpha 1 pulled a dog treat from his jacket, trying to entice Clay forward. The gesture only irritated him further.

"You tryin' to bribe me with a scooby snack?" Clay's internal voice dripped with sarcasm. "If you had a beer or a pizza, we might have a deal, but I don't do tricks for horse jerky."

Alpha 1 grabbed Clay's collar, locked eyes with him, and jabbed a warning finger in his face. The message was clear: behave, or else.

Leaving Clay by the building, Alpha 1 backed away to a safer distance. He signaled to the rest of Alpha team that the dog was in position, then gave Clay the hold signal.

Clay looked side to side and began to ease away, planning his escape. A glance back showed Alpha 1 chambering a round in his assault rifle. Clay froze, mistaking the standard preparation for a threat.

"Alright already," he grumbled internally, returning to his sitting position.

Alpha team moved into strategic positions around the building. SWAT Leader looked up to Delta Leader on the roof, signaling 'in position'. Another mirror flash bounced toward the van.

"All teams in position. Hold for go," Beta Leader's voice crackled through the comms.

Video feeds from inside the factory flickered across monitors. "Hold ... hold ...."

Clay peered at Alpha 1, who still held up the 'hold' signal. Glancing up at the busted window above him, then back at his handler, Clay's anxiety grew. He peeked through a small hole in the wall and his heart nearly stopped — the guards inside were carrying machine guns.

"Point man, GO GO GO!"

Alpha 1 signaled Clay forward, but noticed his K9 was transfixed by something through the hole. He snatched up a small rock and threw it at Clay.

Clay spun around to see Alpha 1 urgently gesturing him forward. He stayed put, fear gripping him.

"I'm sorry, I can't do this," Clay thought. "I'm a varmint control specialist, not a cop."

"Alpha 1! Send the point! Send the point! Go now!"

Alpha 1 aimed his gun at Clay as an escalating incentive to follow orders.

Clay swallowed hard. His handler shook the gun at him, motioning toward the window. Clay looked up, then back at the gun.

"He's not going," Alpha 1 whispered into his comm.

Alpha 1 grabbed another rock and threw it, hitting Clay's back leg before aiming his weapon again.

Clay, with Gabriel's urgent, final messages again echoed through his soul, "Find what you've lost...Find yourself". Making his choice, he darted through it.

Inside the factory, Clay found himself behind a stack of helium and nitrous oxide tanks along the wall. No one had noticed his entry. Nervous and fearful, he crouched down in his hiding place.

Outside, Alpha 1 smacked himself in the head with his pistol. "The point is out of the game. Repeat, the point is out!"

"Dammit!" Beta Leader slammed down his clipboard. After checking his monitors again, he barked, "Engaging contingency plan Hurricane. Alpha team, Delta team, move in!"

The factory erupted into chaos. Delta team members crashed through the upper windows, rappelling down on lines. Concussion grenades flew in from all directions, detonating in blinding flashes.

Alpha team burst through ground-level entry points, catching the criminals by surprise. Both sides drew weapons, creating an instant Mexican standoff.

SWAT Leader strode forward to face the criminal kingpin, who sat at a table covered in cash and balloons.

"Order your men to stand down and you might live to see another day."

The kingpin sneered. "Take you and your boyscouts and leave now. I'll forget this ever happened. Don't, and you'll suffer the consequences."

"Ha! Yeah, right," SWAT Leader scoffed; jabbing an accusatory finger at him. "You don't scare me. I eat rabbit turds like *you* for breakfast!"

Both sides exchanged bewildered looks at this declaration.

"Did he just say he eats turds?" one SWAT member whispered to another.

"Yeah. From a rabbit," the other clarified.

Yet another questioned, "for breakfast?" — as if another time of day might have been proper.

The kingpin and his men erupted in laughter. SWAT Leader paused, reconsidering his words, then played it off by drawing his pistol.

Up on the catwalk, a bad guy crept up behind an unsuspecting Delta team member, grabbing him in a chokehold. The clatter of their struggle rang out loudly across the factory floor.

132

That was all it took. The place exploded into chaos, bullets flying as everyone dove for cover. Gunfire punctured several large helium tanks, releasing jets of gas throughout the warehouse.

Clay tucked his tail and sought deeper cover.

SWAT Leader ducked behind a massive leaking tank and called to his team; his voice now comically high-pitched from the inhaled helium. "C'mon guys, let's get 'em!"

Three thugs charged a SWAT member who was crouching in front of a large canvas-covered object. The officer spun, grabbing the canvas to throw like a net. As he yanked it away, he revealed an antique Circus Wagon with a built-in pipe organ and life-size animatronic clown. The canvas caught the power lever, activating the machine. Suddenly cheerful circus music filled the air as the clown began to animate, its hands jiving back and forth to the tune.

SWAT Leader leaped from behind the tank, guns blazing in both hands as he ran in slow motion to new cover, diving behind a pile of crates.

"Aaaaaaaaaaaaaaagh!" His helium-altered voice shrieked.

Clay panted heavily from his hiding spot, covering his eyes with his paws. As he continued breathing the gas-filled air, his body seemed to become slightly buoyant; almost feeling like he was starting to lift off the ground.

Alpha 2 and some of his teammates took cover behind a stack of boxes. After instructing them, "Cover me!" he attempted a running somersault to another position. But with a half-baked mind at this point, his aim found a pile of inflated balloons and he bounced like a basketball, crashing through a nearby window instead.

The clown continued its absurd dance to the circus music.

Across the way, a SWAT member jumped from behind some nitrous oxide tanks and executed a karate kick on a bad guy. The thug flew back into the wall, bounced off, and slammed back into his attacker. They ricocheted off each other like rubber balls, knocking over more NOS tanks. The tanks' valves snapped off as they hit the ground, releasing clouds of nitrous oxide into the air.

Clay peered from behind a box and spotted a man with a knife sneaking up on Alpha 1, who was unloading his weapon at various targets from behind a crate. One of the NOS tanks in front of Alpha 1 ruptured, giving him a face full of the gas.

Clay began barking in a high-pitched chihuahua voice, trying to warn his handler. The knife-wielding thug grabbed Alpha 1 from behind, pressing the blade to his throat.

"I'm gonna pop you like a balloon, copper!" he squealed, menacingly.

Alpha 1, now high from the gas, burst into hysterical laughter. "Hahahahaha! Oh well. Hahahaha!"

Suddenly the thug dropped his knife, letting out an ultra-high-pitched scream. Clay had his back teeth firmly clamped on the man's buttock. Alpha 1 seized the opportunity and subdued the attacker.

Alpha 1 knelt to praise Clay. "Hahaha! Atta boy! Him is good lil' baby! Hahahaha!"

"Whew! Wow, that was intense!" Clay thought. "Yeah, well, I shoulda let him cut you up. Pointin' guns at a defenseless dog just ain't nice."

Still wide-eyed and panting from the adrenaline rush, Clay sprang into action. He was all-in now. He spotted another thug across the warehouse hiding behind a crate. Clay sprinted forward, launching himself like a missile and bowling the man over.

Alpha 1 witnessed this and celebrated before rejoining the firefight.

Across the way, SWAT Leader, now thoroughly high from the gas filling the warehouse, fixed his attention on the dancing clown still jiving happily to the circus music.

"I hate clowns! Hahaha!"

SWAT Leader took aim and fired. His first shot hit the clown's thumb, blowing it clean off and spinning the hand around. Subsequent shots methodically removed more fingers until only the middle one remained, leaving the clown effectively 'saluting' him to the music. SWAT Leader laughed even harder, but nearby ricochets pulled him back into the action.

Everyone in the building was now blitzed from the mixture of gases. One stumbling thug fired randomly, accidentally striking a natural gas line running up the wall.

A sniper with a rifle lay atop a stack of crates, peering through his scope at the SWAT Leader. Just as his finger tightened on the trigger, he noticed something blocking his view. Pulling back from the scope, he found himself face-to-face with Clay.

Without hesitation, Clay lifted his leg and blinded the sniper with a stream of urine.

"Today's forecast? A hunderd percent chance of showers!" Clay thought triumphantly.

The sniper clutched his burning eyes and rolled off the edge of the crates, crashing to the ground.

The SWAT team continued methodically taking down the bad guys.

SWAT Leader cornered the kingpin, who'd run out of ammo, behind a crate. After laying down suppressing fire, SWAT Leader's gun clicked empty. When the kingpin realized this, he stood, drawing a samurai sword from his back and charging forward.

"Kungfu fightiiiniinng! Hahaha!" the kingpin sang out, his voice drunk from the gas and high-pitched from the helium.

Suddenly, Clay leaped from behind another box and began humping the kingpin's leg as he tried to run. This unexpected attack tripped up the kingpin, who dropped his sword and tumbled to the ground. SWAT Leader quickly moved in to make the arrest.

The Circus Wagon, having taken enough damage, finally sputtered to a halt and its annoying circus music faded as the action wound down. The SWAT team had all the bad guys in custody.

SWAT Leader delivered the cuffed kingpin to another team member.

"All in a day's work," SWAT Leader declared, fishing a cigar from his vest pocket. He placed it between his lips with theatrical flair, reaching for his zippo lighter.

Clay's eyes went wide as saucers as the implications hit him. His keen nose could still detect the cocktail of gases saturating the air — helium, nitrous oxide, and that ruptured natural gas line. One spark and they'd *all* be meeting Gabriel a lot sooner than planned.

"Sweet mercy!" Clay thought in panic. "I ain't ready for another chat with that angel!"

Across the room, Alpha 1's face drained of color as he spotted his commander about to turn them all into a cautionary tale. "NO!" he bellowed, voice still squeaky from the helium. "THE GAS!"

136

But SWAT Leader, ears still ringing from the firefight, just grinned around his cigar, thumb descending toward the lighter's striker.

Clay didn't hesitate. With lightning speed, he launched himself at his commander, jaws clamping down with pinpoint accuracy on a very sensitive target. SWAT Leader let out a falsetto shriek that had nothing to do with helium, the cigar popping from his mouth as he doubled over. The lighter clattered harmlessly to the floor.

Minutes later, outside the factory, the cleanup was in full swing. As officers loaded the last of the perps into a paddy wagon, paramedics wheeled SWAT Leader to an ambulance. He lay on the stretcher, hands cupped protectively over his injured groin.

Alpha 1 approached the stretcher, layering on the concern so thick you could spread it with a knife. "Oh sir, this is just terrible! Please get well soon — the team won't be the same without your ... unique leadership style." Behind his sympathetic expression, though, his eyes danced with barely contained glee. Nothing like seeing a pompous windbag taken down a few notches, especially by man's best friend.

Once the ambulance pulled away, Alpha 1's facade cracked. He turned to Clay with an ear-splitting grin, dropping to one knee and vigorously scratching behind the dog's ears. "Who's a good boy? Who just saved everybody from becoming ceiling decoration — and gave that blowhard exactly what he deserves? You did! Yes, you did!"

Clay endured the baby-talk with dignity, knowing he'd done the right thing. Even if it meant taking a bite out of crime in a rather ... unconventional way.

Just then, Beta Leader's voice came across Alpha 1's comm link. "Alpha 1, got forensics requesting your K9 unit."

Still chuckling and patting his furry hero, Alpha1 confirmed, "Copy."

Clay sat in the back of a police squad car as Officer 1 pulled up to his half-blown-up home.

"Hey, my house. Perfect!" he thought, recognizing his destination.

The officer retrieved Clay from the car. "C'mon, boy."

In the backyard, a large wood chipper stood in the corner, set up in preparation to clean up the fallen tree. The officer gestured around the yard, instructing Clay to sniff for evidence.

"Take a look around, buddy. See if you can find a trace of the explosive."

Clay looked at the officer with barely concealed exasperation. "Oh, that's easy, it was moonshine," he thought, but all the officer heard was a soft rumble.

"Now!" the officer commanded, growing impatient.

Clay turned toward the shed. He made a deliberate 'point' to the general area, not bothering to even pretend to sniff around.

The officer scratched his head, clearly frustrated. "What is wrong with you today? You didn't even sniff anything." He walked over to the shed. "In here?"

After letting Clay into the shed, the officer watched as his K9 immediately 'pointed' at the moonshine still. Pulling on surgical gloves, the officer prepared to examine the evidence, but his frustration with Clay's unusual behavior was evident.

"Alright, that does it. You're done. Just go outside and relax if you know what's good for you. I'll deal with you later."

Clay retreated as requested and found a shady spot to lie down. Through a gap in the fence, he could see Sampson roaming his neighbor's yard.

"Well if it isn't the infamous duck killer, Sampson," he thought bitterly. "Bully!"

Sampson pranced over and sniffed at the fence, sensing Clay's presence. As the dog followed the fence line in Clay's direction, a strange rattling sound caught Clay's attention. Peering through another crack, he spotted a rattlesnake coiled in defense, preparing for Sampson's approach.

Sampson heard the warning rattle and turned his attention to the snake. He began to bark, pawing and nipping at the deadly reptile, which struck back with several near misses.

The snake maneuvered closer to the fence to escape Sampson's harassment. In that moment, Clay made his choice. With lightning speed, he grabbed the snake's tail through the fence and yanked it backward. While shaking the rattler violently in his jaws and juiced up on adrenalin, Clay didn't even notice that the serpent sunk its fangs briefly into his rump. But he persisted, whipping it side-to-side like a wet rag doll. Flinging it across his yard, the snake quickly retreated under the back fence and out of sight.

Clay turned his attention back to his former nemesis. "I shoulda let him bite you, Sampson. It would serve you rightly. But, you're welcome."

Suddenly, Clay felt an overwhelming wave of fatigue wash over him. He lay down, his limbs growing inexplicably heavy.

"Mmmm, wow, feeling really tired," he thought hazily. "What's going on here?"

"Oh, Maddie," he thought, his mind growing fuzzy. "Why didn't we ever get our chance together? I know we were just kids when we first met, but you've turned out to be even more than I could imagine. I think I ... I ...."

Clay's head lowered to the grass as his consciousness began to fade. His eyes drifted shut, the world growing dim around him.

12 - Illumination

Clay slowly faded back into his human form, the ethereal expanse of Heaven giving way to a familiar scene. He looked over at Gabriel who stood solemnly by the candle — the flame now just a flicker atop a puddle of melted wax. Suddenly, deep alarms began to sound, echoing through the vastness.

Clay walked over to stand behind Gabriel, who didn't turn to greet him. The angel's silence was unnerving.

"Gabriel, don't end this. I'm not ready. I'm still broken. Give me another chance. Send me back. Please!" Clay pleaded, desperation rising in his voice. "I'll even go back as a cat. Heck, send me back as a worm, a gnat, anything."

Gabriel turned, fixing Clay with a piercing stare that seemed to bore into his very soul. Unspoken volumes passed between them in that weighted gaze.

The angel motioned to the figures in the distance. Clay watched in disbelief as Pete and the others waiting in line hurriedly packed up the disassembled gates into the back of a pickup truck. The heavenly hosts shed their gowns, revealing ordinary street-clothes beneath.

"No! No, I don't want to go!" Clay cried out, anguish twisting his features. "I want to live!"

But the light was fading, the world dimming around him until only the weak glow of the guttering candle remained. Gabriel's form shimmered and vanished, leaving Clay alone in the gathering darkness.

Hyperventilating, Clay rushed to cup his hands around the fragile flame, as if he could shelter it from a nonexistent wind. "Don't go out," he whispered frantically. "Don't go ...."

Silence fell like a heavy curtain; darkness absolute. For a stretching eternity, there was nothing. No sound, no light, no sensation. Nothing.

Then, so gradually it was almost imperceptible at first, a low rumbling began, rising in strength and volume until it was a deafening roar. Light exploded back into being, searing in its intensity. Clay screamed, shielding his eyes, gasping like a drowning man finally breaching the surface.

He fell to his knees, shaking with great, wracking sobs as he beheld the source of the light. There, standing before him, was the Creator Himself, radiant and barely distinguishable in the brilliance that emanated from His form.

Peeking through his fingers, Clay gazed up at the figure, awe and terror warring in his chest. But as he looked, really looked, a profound peace settled over him like a warm mantle. His hands fell away from his face, tears still streaming down his cheeks.

"I've made a mess of things, haven't I?" Clay said, his voice trembling but sure. "I've neglected life itself. But I don't know what to do. It's been so long for me like this."

He swallowed hard, forcing himself to confront the painful truth. "Even when I have a bright moment from time to time, I just can't seem to pull it all together. I scare myself. It scares me what sort of evil I can do. I need help. I need *your* help. I can't do it myself. I want to be happy like I was. I need help like an armless man needs slip-on shoes."

The bright light flickered, as if in sympathetic amusement at Clay's analogy. Emboldened, he pressed on.

Clay met the Creator's gaze with growing clarity. "You know what? I finally understand why y'all kept sendin' me back as different critters. Had to make me walk in their paws, didn't ya? Because I never showed 'em a lick of respect." He let out a shaky breath. "I treated God's creatures like they was nothin' but problems to be solved. Turns out I was the real varmint all along."

The light pulsed gently, encouraging him to continue.

"And that fella Bruce?" Clay's voice softened with shame. "When I first met him, I labeled him right quick, just like I done to everyone else who wasn't exactly like me. But that man showed me nothing but kindness, even when I was acting like a dadjim fool." He ran a hand over his face. "I was so busy judgin' others, I never stopped to look in the mirror. Maybe that's why you had me see all them reflections of myself — as a cockroach, a duck, a gerbil. Made me see how it feels to be on the other side of someone's judgment."

Clay shifted on his knees, the weight of understanding settling deeper into his bones. "And Maddie ... sweet mercy, Maddie had it right all along. While I was stuffin' myself with moonshine and pride, worryin' about my own hurts and wants, she was out there carin' for every living thing that crossed her path. She understood what you made this world for. She respected your creation in a way I never did."

The light grew warmer, and Clay felt tears rolling down his cheeks again. "That's what was in her letter, wasn't it? That's what Gabriel was trying to tell me. It wasn't about the paper at all — it was about the heart behind it — Maddie's heart — I get that now. The way she loves everything and everyone, no questions asked."

He looked down at his trembling hands. "I've been chasin' that letter like it was some kind of magical fix, when really, I should've been chasin' the truth inside of it. The truth about how to live. How to love." His voice cracked. "How to be the person Maddie saw in me all those years ago."

The Creator's presence seemed to envelop him, and Clay felt decades of hardness melting away from his heart.

"Ya know what's funny?" he said, his voice barely above a whisper. "When I was busy bein' all them different animals, there were moments — just moments — when I'd forget myself and do something good without thinkin' about it. Like saving my SWAT buddy, or even that dadjim dog Sampson. In those moments, I wasn't worried about what was in it for me. I just ... did what needed doin'."

The bright light pulsed again, warming Clay to his core.

"I think I'm finally gettin' it," he said, wonder creeping into his voice. "Life ain't about what we can take from it. It ain't about judgin' others or provin' we're better than them. It's about," he paused, searching for the words. "It's about bein' part of something bigger than ourselves. Every creature, even that ornery armadilla, has its place in your plan."

Clay sat back on his heels, a lifetime of understanding washing over him. "You know what's really got me feelin' foolish? All this time I been blamin' you for takin' people away from me, when really, you was just tryin' to show me how precious every moment is. Every breath. Every chance to do right by someone else."

144

The light flickered, as if in gentle agreement.

"Life is precious...." Clay began, but suddenly the light grew blindingly bright and pulsed with tremendous force. A deep rumble shook through him as distant voices began to filter through the brilliance.

"Clear!" a voice echoed.

The light pulsed again, synchronized with a thunderous thump that rattled Clay's very bones. He flinched at the impact.

"What is that?" he asked, fear edging into his voice. "What's going on?"

The voices grew more urgent, then another command: "Clear!"

Another pulse, another bone-jarring thump. Clay's body jerked with the force of it. Medical equipment began beeping in the distance, the sound growing clearer with each passing second.

The light surrounding Clay grew impossibly brighter, until it consumed everything — the darkness, the emptiness, even Clay himself. As his consciousness began to fade into the white brilliance, his last thought was of gratitude — not just for another chance at life, but for finally understanding what life truly meant. He realized he couldn't do it all himself; he needed others. And he needed to do his part to help others too; to love his neighbor. And to love his Creator, and be grateful for life itself, and to rest in and to rely on mercy.

The blinding whiteness slowly began to recede, resolving into the beam of a penlight being flashed across his eyes. A doctor's face swam into focus above him.

"He's back," Dr. Revida announced, relief evident in her voice. "He's back with us."

The steady beeping of hospital monitors filled the air. Clay lay in a hospital bed, his body wrapped in bandages, as the doctor lowered her stethoscope and pulled down her mask.

"Can you hear me, Ordell?" she asked. "Can you squeeze my finger?"

Through his blurred vision, Clay saw the doctor turn to speak to someone else in the room. "I'm not sure why he crashed; that was highly unusual. But he's back with us now."

Then a face he'd know anywhere appeared above him — Maddie, her eyes brimming with tears of relief.

"Clay? Oh, thank God," she breathed. "You gave us a scare!"

Pastor Matt moved into view on Clay's other side. The two of them, Maddie and Matt, stood vigil as Clay struggled to focus, to force words past his parched throat.

"What's that, honey?" Maddie leaned in close, her ear nearly brushing his cracked lips. "What are you trying to say?"

"Sweet. Mercy," Clay whispered, the familiar words carrying a weight they've never held before; not of surprise or frustration, but profound gratitude and wonder. His voice cracked with emotion as tears gathered in his eyes. "Sweet ... Mercy."

Maddie's fingers were cool and gentle as they combed through Clay's singed hair. With what felt like a monumental effort, he turned his head to meet her tear-bright gaze.

"Sunshine," he whispered, summoning a ghost of a smile.

Then his eyes slid over to Pastor Matt, standing steadfast on his other side. "Friend."

146

The pastor returned his smile, warm and genuine. "Welcome back, pal. You've been in a coma for the past several weeks. It's good to see life in your eyes again."

Clay let his head fall back against the pillow, gratitude and exhaustion warring in his battered body. But when his gaze found Maddie's again, he saw a telltale glint of mischief sparkling there.

"Matt filled me in on some things while you were out," she said, arching an eyebrow playfully. "Sounds like you've been a bad little boy since I last saw you."

Clay huffed out a weak chuckle, even as remorse twisted in his gut. "You have no idea, Maddie. I've done some terrible things. Just terrible. And I lost my lust for life." He reached out, clasping her hand in his. She squeezed back, her grip warm and sure.

"But I got a second chance," Clay said, determination threading through his wavering voice. "And I ain't gonna waste it. Life is a gift. Every day, a gift. And if you'll have me, I'd love to work through some things. With your help."

Maddie's smile was like the break of dawn after the longest, darkest night. "Well, as long as you don't want me to help you build a clubhouse, I suppose that'd be okay. I seem to recall your carpentry skills left something to be desired."

Clay barked out a laugh, wincing as his ribs protested. But the pain was nothing compared to the joy, the sweet relief, of Maddie's teasing words. She hadn't abandoned him; in spite of what he'd become over the years. She didn't throw him away like a lost cause; that was Maddie … and that's who *he* wanted to be.

Moments later, a familiar figure bustled into the room — Bruce, clad in hospital scrubs and brandishing a sponge. "Welcome back, Slugger! Time for another spongebaaath!"

Clay blinked, uncomprehending. His gaze darted from Bruce's beaming face to Maddie, a mute plea for rescue, for explanation.

But Maddie just smiled, a little quirk of her lips that held a thousand unspoken promises.

Slowly, inevitably, Clay felt his own mouth curve in response. A grin tugged at the corners, spreading wider and wider until it crinkled the corners of his eyes.

He was alive. Maddie was here. And maybe, just *maybe*, that was enough.

The future stretched out before him, a blank page waiting to be filled. A chance to make things right. To be the man he was always meant to be. To rely on forgiveness and mercy.

It wouldn't be easy. Change never was. But with Maddie by his side, with the hard-won wisdom of his trials etched into his heart ... well, stranger things had happened.

As Bruce advanced, sponge at the ready, Clay offered his grateful hand and gave Bruce a welcoming shake, "Thank you, buddy."

Through the hospital room's window, Clay noticed a strange presence — a stork perched on the narrow sill, staring at him. Before taking wing into the evening sky, the majestic bird gave what might have been a blink, or perhaps a final wink of approval.

Clay couldn't help but wonder if Gabriel was checking in on him one last time, but the thought only made his smile grow wider. He closed his eyes, letting the laughter rise up like a healing spring — deep, genuine, and full of newfound joy.

It felt like hope.

It felt like ... love.

John 13:34

Matthew 22: 37-39

"Sometimes God puts gold under my shovel, so I dig."

Matthew W Bertsch (1968) was born and raised in Fort Wayne, Indiana.

From an early age, Matthew loved to create. He spent much of his free time capturing stories on his mother's cassette recorder. In high school he focused his creativity on producing video shorts, winning First Place at the Indiana State Media Fair and Honorable Mention at a National Competition in Atlanta, Georgia.

In 1992, Matthew earned a Bachelor's Degree in Telecommunications (specializing in writing) from Purdue University in West Lafayette, Indiana. His poem "Heritage" was published in the 1992 Purdue Exponent Literary Issue.

Matthew's second book, 'Carnation: The Many Lives of Ordell Clayton Hart, centers on the daily struggle to be mindful of loving your neighbor.